Let Love In

MacKay Family Generations

By Karen Kinney

Copyright © 2024 Karen Kinney All rights reserved.

The characters and events portrayed in this book are fictitious. Any similarity to real persons, living or dead, is coincidental and not intended by the author.

No part of this book may be reproduced, or stored in a retrieval system, or transmitted in any form or by any means, electronic, mechanical, photocopying, recording, or otherwise, without express written permission of the publisher

ISBN: 979-8-9901998-2-8

Cover by Linda Irvine

To the memory of Phillip, my husband of more than 36 years: The day you left this life for your heavenly home was the first of many hard days for me, but I'm so thankful that we shared a faith in God and the confidence that death is not the end when we trust our lives to Jesus. Without that assurance, I would have been so lost. I miss you every day, but I know I will see you again in heaven, and I continue to pray that our whole family will be there with us. Thank you for leading our family with Christian values

And to Dennis: Thank you for your friendship and your wisdom while helping me gain perspective in many things as we both navigate our grief.

And to the leaders of the ladies Bible study for helping me better understand that Satan's lies do not define me.

Contents

CHAPTER ONE	1
CHAPTER TWO	13
CHAPTER THREE	26
CHAPTER FOUR	37
CHAPTER FIVE	49
CHAPTER SIX	62
CHAPTER SEVEN	79
CHAPTER EIGHT	91
CHAPTER NINE	103
CHAPTER TEN	116
CHAPTER ELEVEN	130
CHAPTER TWELVE	145
CHAPTER THIRTEEN	158
CHAPTER FOURTEEN	174
CHAPTER FIFTEEN	190
CHAPTER SIXTEEN	209
CHAPTER SEVENTEEN	222
CHAPTER EIGHTEEN	238
CHAPTER NINETEEN	250
CHAPTER TWENTY	267
CHAPTER TWENTY-ONE	282
CHAPTER TWENTY-TWO	294
CHAPTER TWENTY-THREE	308
CHAPTER TWENTY-FOUR	321
CHAPTER TWENTY-FIVE	335
CHAPTER TWENTY-SIX	352
EPILOGUE	371

Chapter One

Spring, 1820 - Northwestern North Carolina

James MacKay whistled a merry tune under a cloudless blue spring sky as he coaxed his bay gelding along the road. He was finally heading home! The past few months had made him weary, and he had decided that it was time to end this part of his life, traveling from one town to another on the circuit, month after month, year after year. He missed his family, so it was best for him to return to his roots, back where it all began.

He mentally calculated how long it had been since he was last home. It was fifteen years since he had lived there, but his last visit was just last year for his youngest brother's wedding. He had been honored to perform the marriage ceremonies of five of his siblings over the past few years, and the last one would be next month. Being the eldest of seven, he had gone away long before most of them were old enough to leave home.

How had it been fifteen years already? Emily Rose had been not much more than a toddler then, and now she was getting married. James was starting to feel his age. He adored each of his siblings, and loved their spouses, also. His nieces and nephews were a lot of fun whenever they were all gathered at the plantation, but he always felt the loss of what could have been. What should have been.

No, he would not allow his thoughts to go there. He was enjoying the day and refused to allow dark thoughts and memories of the past to cast shadows and dampen the mood. Instead, he would focus on what was to come. According to his calculations, he should be home by tomorrow afternoon. It would be good to be home. He could not wait to tell his family that his traveling days were over, and that he would be establishing a law practice in their hometown. He could imagine his mother's elation when she learned he would not be leaving for work anymore. And getting reacquainted with the family and friends he didn't often see on his regular visits would be wonderful.

Home. Growing up on Jessup Plantation had been a great adventure. It was hard work, but between their large family and all the workers who lived on the property, it was almost like living in a small town. His father, who was born and raised in the Scottish Highlands, came to America as a farmer, and after he was injured in the war, found himself at Jessup Plantation in North Carolina. His grandmother had convinced him that she needed him to take over running the plantation, and though he was reluctant to go along with her tactics, he agreed.

Manipulated. That's what she had done. Because she knew she was dying, she selected James' father to protect the Jessup legacy. The details surrounding her reasons for what she did seemed questionable to James, and he wondered if a court would uphold the wishes of his grandparents if his parents had not fallen in love in spite of the circumstances.

James was sad that he never met any of his grandparents, but he thought his parents had done very well considering they were so young when their parents died. He was grateful they were still alive and healthy, and that they were a steadfast presence for his brothers and sisters, as well as for all their grandchildren. James had a sense of pride when thinking about his family. His parents were loving and kind and had taught all their children to love the Lord. They set a wonderful example as Christians, both in the community as well as at home.

Most of the MacKay clan still lived close to home, and James was glad for that. He couldn't imagine any of them living somewhere else. In fact, James was the only one who had ventured so far away. At one time, he had been part of a local law practice, and his life was wonderful. He had a beautiful, loving wife, and they had anticipated the birth of their first child with great joy. However, nothing could have prepared them for what happened. The baby, a boy they named John, died during birth, and because of complications, Victoria had lost so much blood that she soon followed her son in death.

The whole family had been devastated, but no one more than James. In fact, in an effort to get away from all that was familiar, he took some time away from home, trying to clear his head. At the age of twenty two, he suddenly found himself alone again after spending three short years with the woman he expected to love for the rest of his life. They had such plans! They had just finished building their dream house on the edge of town, and planned to fill it with love, laughter, and children. At the time, James struggled to understand how God could have let such a thing happen to them when they were just getting started. But since it was too painful to remain in town, he left.

Shortly after, James encountered a man who helped change his life. That man was a judge who showed him how much he could help smaller towns farther from the city and in the mountains as a traveling judge, coming around on a regular schedule, giving legal guidance, settling disputes, performing marriages, attending to other legal matters, and assisting local law enforcement. So, James became a judge and did exactly that. It had been the change he needed at the time.

Over the fifteen years he had been on the circuit, he met a lot of interesting people and saw some beautiful scenery. He enjoyed watching the seasons change from one to the next, and he especially loved how majestic the mountains were, no matter the season. He had a reputation for being fair and decisive, and had developed a good rapport with the people.

His circuit took approximately three months to complete, so he saw each place four times a year. During this time, he had seen a lot of changes in people, watched children grow up and fall in love, performed marriages where ministers were not available, and settled disputes of land ownership, among other things. Usually, the job was simple and enjoyable, but recently there had been a few reports of trouble in the foothills, mostly around mining towns. He hoped his replacement would be able to get to the bottom of it and help the people he had grown to love.

Several months ago, he realized he was weary of the life he was leading and had grown restless. He visited his friend and mentor in the city where he learned of a young man, Roger Jefferies, who was eager for a new challenge, so he brought him on his rounds to teach him about the people and their ways. He was a bright, energetic, and kind young man, and James was content that he was leaving things in competent hands. And now, he was glad to be going home to stay. It was time.

The sun had dropped low enough in the sky to make the shadowy figures that were him and his horse appear long and thin. James began to wonder if he would need to spend the night camping when the familiar shape of Orchard Grove came into view. He knew he should be getting close, as this was the last town on his circuit. Whenever he was in this area, he tried to take a couple of extra days to see his family, but this time he was not in town for work. Hopefully there was a room available for him tonight at the boarding house. He could use a hot meal and a good bed.

Things were quiet as he rode down the main street toward the boarding house. Mrs. Fields would likely be surprised to see him as this was not the usual time for him to be in town. He grinned, remembering the playful banter he had with the older lady who could have been his grandmother. She was tiny, barely over five feet tall, but she had boundless energy for someone her age. And she was a fantastic cook. His mouth watered at the thought of eating one of her hot meals tonight. He knew that even if all the rooms were full, she would make a place for him at her table. And if she didn't have a room for him, it wouldn't be the first time he camped out with his horse.

The warm light shining through the windows of the dining room told him that people would soon be seated there, so he hurried to the livery stable to take care of his horse.

"Judge MacKay! I didn't know you was coming to town this month. Here, let me take care of Justice for you," the young stable master said as he approached with a smile.

Returning the greeting with a smile of his own, James said, "Thank you, Andrew. I appreciate it! I'm on my way over to see if Mrs. Fields has enough food to share for dinner tonight. If you need me, that's where I'll be."

"You know she will come up with something since it's you." Andrew grinned. People in this town were like family to James, and they all went out of their way to show their appreciation. He would miss them, but since they were less than a day's ride from Jessup Plantation, there was no reason he couldn't visit occasionally. With a wave, he left the stable and walked the two blocks to the boarding house.

A huge smile lit Mrs. Fields' face when she opened the door to him a few minutes later.

"James, my dear boy, what are you doing here?" Then, waving her hand in a dismissive way, and giving him a grandmotherly hug, she continued. "Never mind, it doesn't matter! I'm just so happy to see you, as always! Are ya hungry?"

James chuckled. She was always the same. "You know I am! I was hoping you had saved me some of your delicious stew and a nice piece of apple pie."

"I always have something special for my favorite judge," she said with a wink. Laughing together, they made their way to the kitchen. They stood chatting for a few minutes while she put the finishing touches on dinner. James naturally pitched in to help, getting the rolls out of the oven for her, and filling a pitcher with lemonade then placing it on the table. "So, how is your family? I'll bet you are on your way to see them, what with Emily Rose's wedding coming up soon and all. They will be so happy to see you."

"Yes, I am on my way there for her wedding, but there is more. Do you remember a few months ago when a young man was with me? We didn't want to say much at the time, but I am retiring from the circuit, and he will be taking over. I'm weary from living my life on the back of a horse." James chuckled at the vision his comment conjured.

Mrs. Fields nearly dropped her ladle as she whirled to face him. Her previously twinkling eyes were suddenly watery, and James' heart dropped to his belly. He had come to love this lady like a matriarchal member of his own family. It broke his heart to see her upset, so he gathered her in for a warm embrace. "My home is not so far away that I can't come see you. Promise that if you are ever in need of anything, you send for me. I will only be a short ride away. Promise?"

He felt her nod against his chest, and for the first time since he began plans to leave the circuit, he was sad; sad that he may not be seeing this dear lady as frequently. He would need to arrange to come back as often as possible.

"So, what will you do now that you're leaving the circuit?" she asked after she got her emotions in check.

"I plan to set up a new practice in Jessup, several miles west of Greensboro, which makes it much closer to here if you need me. It is the town closest to my family's plantation. I am ready to settle down and stay in one place for most of the year."

"I guess I don't need to tell you that I will miss your regular visits. I will expect the new man to stay here like you always have." Giving him a skeptical look, she asked, "What should I know about him?"

"Roger is young and eager, bright and intelligent. He's a good man and has a good head on his shoulders. Just give him a chance; you will learn to love him as you have me," James replied with a wink.

In mock exasperation, she swatted at him and said, "Who said anything about love? You young pups don't know anything." He caught her smirk as she turned back to the stove, just as guests began filtering in to sit at the table.

Chapter Two

James could tell that Mrs. Fields was subdued, not her normal jovial self. It saddened him that his news had that effect on her, but he wanted to be the one to tell her. He didn't want her to worry about him not coming around four times a year like he had been for the last fifteen years. He had a lot of respect and affection for the elderly lady. He decided that if she ever needed care, he would take her to his own home and provide for her. She had been nothing but good to him all these years. They had an easy camaraderie that he hadn't always found in the other towns.

Yes, people had accepted him everywhere, but there was something special about Orchard Grove, and Mrs. Fields was one of those things. If it ever came to it, he knew his family would accept her with open arms as an honorary member of their family. Over the years he had learned that her husband, Gus, had passed away long ago, and her only daughter, Susie, had died from smallpox as a child. As he came to know her better those first few visits, he felt drawn to her in a way he had not felt with any of the other people he met.

James listened to the conversation amongst the other guests, joining in occasionally. It was surprising what a person could learn just by listening to people talk. He had a lot on his mind, so he didn't banter with the other men or Mrs. Fields like he usually did. Still, he kept one ear open. Sometimes he had been able to glean information people would not normally offer when they discovered he was a judge. Amazing how that little fact closed mouths.

His thoughts started to wander to the next day and to his anticipated arrival back at the plantation. He smiled to himself, knowing the excitement his family would demonstrate when he arrived a full two weeks ahead of schedule. His imagination was painting the happy picture when his mind caught a few words from the other end of the table.

"Something should be done about this; people are being forced out of their homes. There ain't no reason for it. I know of a few women who have been forced to leave just 'cause someone wants the property they were left by their husbands. It happens more often up at the mining camps, but I'm sure it's happening just about anywhere. Ain't there a law to protect these people?"

Mrs. Fields glanced at James. She knew he liked to protect his identity unless there was reason to reveal it. He met her gaze with a quick wink and turned to the man who had been talking.

"Do you have any idea who is putting pressure on them?"

"No, I don't. I travel around to the different mining camps, checking on their records and such, making sure everything is in order, and I hear things. It sounds like there's several men who are dressed in fine suits, masquerading as authority. I wish someone would find them and put a stop to it. These poor people should not be forced from their homes."

"Has the marshal been notified?"

"Yes, and several deputies have been added to help try and locate these men. Personally, I think they are criminals who are hiding up in the hill country. When they hear that one of the miners has died, they make their move on the grieving widow. It's just a shame!"

"Yes, it does sound like it," James agreed. This is exactly the trouble he had heard was going on this past year. He wondered if any men were being forced out if their wives died, or if it was only women who were being targeted. He would send Roger a telegram in the morning with this new information. Hopefully these men would be caught and brought to justice soon.

Another man spoke up. "It happened to a woman in my hometown just last week. The man presented her with official looking papers that said she had three days to vacate the premises if she didn't sign. Her husband had just died the week before, and she was terrified. That poor woman!"

"Wow. I wonder where she went." James tried to get the information he needed without seeming overly interested. He would be more likely to get damning evidence if people did not know what he could do.

"I heard she came here to Orchard Grove to stay with her brother's family." James' eyes slid over to meet those of Mrs. Fields. An almost imperceptible twitch of her eyebrow told him she knew something. He usually stayed after dinner to help her clean up, and tonight would be no different. His mind went to work, making a list of things to check on. First thing, after questioning Mrs. Fields, of course, was to track down the local sheriff to see what he knew.

Mrs. Fields rose from her chair and began clearing plates and carrying them to the kitchen. Gradually the men who were staying there thanked her for the wonderful meal, and either left the house or went to their rooms. James gathered platters and serving bowls, taking them to the kitchen where Mrs. Fields put together the customary plates for the sheriff and any prisoners he had in the jail. "I'll be happy to take those over to the jail for you after we get this cleaned up," James told her. He was surprised to see a nervous smile as his answer.

"Alright, what's going on? Tell me what you know."

She averted her eyes. "I don't know what you mean."

"Do you really think I don't know you better than that? I know that talk about the women being forced from their homes affected you. Please, tell me what's going on. Has someone put pressure on you? Do you know who the woman is who came to Orchard Grove? Talk to me. I can help."

With a deep sigh and worried eyes, she turned to face him. "A few weeks ago, a distinguished looking man came and stayed for a few days. He seemed friendly enough, and we had several pleasant conversations, sometimes over coffee or tea, sometimes on the porch. He started asking a lot of questions about how I came to be here, where my husband was, why I stayed after he died, and so on. He was so easy to talk to, almost like you, and I started to trust him. He talked like he wanted to help me, saying he understood how difficult it must be to maintain a place this size, and that he knew people who were available to work on repairs and such in exchange for room and board. He gave me documents, saying that if I signed them, he'd get the man here to do the work, but I refused to do that. When I hesitated, he started getting gruff. It looked like he was trying hard to keep his anger under control, so I went to my room and locked the door. But I wasn't born yesterday, you know. I can see through people most of the time. Anyway, that night when I took dinner to the sheriff, I told him about what had happened. He told me not to sign anything until he or someone I trust could take a look at the documents. The next day that man left."

James let out a breath he didn't realize he was holding. "I'm glad you didn't sign anything. Do you still have the documents?"

"Yes, of course. He wanted to get them back from me, but I had locked them in my room. Besides, how was I to know if I should sign them unless I read them over first? He eventually gave up. They're right here." She went to a corner cabinet and removed a folded bundle of papers from a drawer, handing them to James. "I think I know the woman they were talking about. Her name is Gretchen, I believe. Her brother owns a farm about two miles north of town. His name is Gunther Schmidt. I talked to her the other day for a few minutes at the mercantile. She seemed so sad, but I didn't know why. She wouldn't say much, even to me!"

James chuckled. He could imagine her indignation at not getting that poor woman to immediately become her friend. He put an arm around Mrs. Fields and dropped a kiss on top of her snowy white head. "Thank you for the information. It might be important in catching whoever is doing this. I'm going to go have a talk with the sheriff. Is this all you want to send over there?"

"Yes, as far as I know, no one is in jail right now, but there's an extra serving just in case. James, I'm glad you're here. I feel safer knowing you are around."

"I'm glad too. And remember, I'll be easier to find now, just up the road a few miles." He smiled and winked, then turned to go.

***

The sheriff's office was just up the block and around the corner from Mrs. Field's boarding house. It was a pleasant evening, and normally James would take his time, noticing any changes made around town since his last visit here, but this evening he had an agenda. He shifted the plates to his left hand and opened the door with his right, stepping into the dimly lit room.

"Well, well, well, Judge MacKay. What are you doing in town? You're not due here for another month, are ya?" Sheriff Matt O'Connor stood with a smile, stretching out a hand toward James.

"Sheriff, how have you been?" James smiled and returned the friendly handshake. "I'm just passing through this time. On my way home for my little sister's wedding, but I'm staying there for good."

Matt's eyebrows snapped up to the edge of his hat. "Is that right?! I never thought you'd give up the good life."

James laughed. "It's time. My backside is tired of sitting on a horse all the time. I'll miss people and scenery, but I miss my family more. I'm going to start a private law practice in Jessup. Just don't tell my mama yet. I'd like to do that myself."

Matt laughed. "I'm guessing you'll see her before I do, so your secret is safe with me. So, what's new? You can fill me in while I eat this delicious smelling dinner. That woman sure can cook, can't she?" He sat down behind his desk and tucked into the meal on the plate while James told him a few tales of his travels over the last few weeks. When he was close to finishing his meal, he looked up at James and saw the crease that wrinkled his brow. "What's got you bothered, my friend?"

James chuckled and met his gaze. Friends like Matt knew him pretty well, so he got straight to the point. "A few weeks ago, we were made aware of some trouble, mostly in the mining towns, but tonight a few of the guests at the boarding house talked about some incidents they've either heard of or witnessed, close by. After dinner, I asked Mrs. Fields what she knew, and her answer both surprised and distressed me." He told Matt everything he had heard and what Mrs. Fields had told him, then asked him if he knew anything about it.

The sheriff sighed and rubbed the tension from the back of his neck. "You know we have to be cautious about acting on every complaint. Much of the time it's a wild goose chase, and I don't have the manpower to follow up in detail to everything. However, Mrs. Fields did talk to me about the guest at the boarding house. I gave her concern a little more attention than most because of who she is, but I came up empty. I wish I had more to go on, more than a description of her guest, but there just isn't anything." He blew out a breath. "Anyone scarin' widow ladies is lower than a snake's belly in my opinion. There's just nothin' legally I can do yet."

"I understand. But did you know a woman recently was forced from her home and came here for refuge at her brother's farm?"

"I heard there was a new woman around, but I haven't had cause to talk to her. What do you know?"

"Only what the guest tonight said. And what Mrs. Fields filled in. She met her at the mercantile, but she said the woman was pretty close lipped. For Mrs. Fields not to be able to make an immediate friend, she's either pretty spooked or just plain shy. She did give me a name, though. Maybe you could go visit her?"

"I'll try to go see her in the morning. You want to ride out with me?"

"Guess I could. I had hoped to get home by midafternoon, but if we can find out what's going on, the delay would be worth it."

"I wouldn't want to make your mama unhappy, now. I can send a messenger to you when I know more if that would be better."

James grinned. "I'm a full two weeks ahead of when they are expecting me, so I have time. I wouldn't stay if Mrs. Fields hadn't been approached by that scum, though. She's like everybody's grandmother, and I feel like I need to protect her, you know?"

"I know, brother. I feel the same way. Alright then, how about I come by the boarding house for breakfast and invite you to take a ride with me? We don't want to raise suspicions, just in case one of the men staying there reports back to the ringleader. I want to get to the bottom of this, find out why women are being targeted and what the perpetrator gets out of it. Oh, and ask Mrs. Fields to let you keep those documents he wanted her to sign. I want to have a look at them."

"Right. I intend to take a closer look myself when I get to my room." Standing, he reached out to shake the other man's hand. "Thanks, Matt. I appreciate all you do. See you in the morning."

Chapter Three

Olivia Martin attempted to dry her cheeks as she knelt beside her husband's grave. She wondered if there would ever come a day when the tears no longer fell. Right now, she was sure that would never happen. She had shed so many already, it was hard to believe there were any left. It had been four months now since Peter died unexpectedly, leaving her alone with their two children.

Oh, Peter...why did you leave me? What did I do wrong to make God take you from me? Don't you know how much I need you? I need your strength and wisdom, I need your love and support, I need your comfort and protection. I miss you so desperately! I understand now how people die of a broken heart, but you know I won't...I can't, because we have Frannie and Michael who still need their parents. I don't know how I can do that without you, though. They need their father. I'm struggling to keep things normal for the sake of the children, but I'm afraid they can see through my efforts. What am I going to do? I'm trying my best, but I fear I'm failing them. How can I be strong for them when I feel myself falling apart? I wish you could tell me how to do this!

It seems like people in town have already forgotten you and are going on with life as if nothing has changed, but the world as I knew it has ended. I'm afraid I will forget the sound of your voice, your laugh, your breathing as you sleep. I miss your touch and the way you made me feel cherished. I don't remember the last time I laughed, truly laughed. I see and hear things that remind me of you, and the tears start all over again. I loved you so much, and I hope you never doubted that, my darling.

She sat there for several more minutes until she was able to regain composure, then she kissed her fingers and allowed them to linger on the stone at the head of his grave. Slowly, she rose from her knees and made her way to the gate that opened at the edge of the street.

As cemeteries go, this was a nice one. It was well laid out and had pretty trees and flowers in strategic locations. All the grave markers were in straight lines. She had seen some cemeteries that were sloppy and haphazard, and she was grateful she had been able to bury Peter in this one instead.

As she approached the street, she became aware of someone walking toward her. Glancing up, she noticed a man in a dark coat and hat. She was not necessarily reserved, but neither was she overly friendly, especially with people she did not know, so she continued on her way without a word.

"Pardon me, ma'am. Was that your husband's grave you were visiting? I'm sorry to be so forward. It's just that the loss of a loved one is so new to me, I wonder how other people manage."

His words startled her, and she stopped and looked up at him as he was now only about ten feet away from her. How had she not noticed someone else in the cemetery when she came in? She felt a little unnerved, especially since no one knew she was here. She tried to be discreet when coming because she didn't want the children to worry about her, and she certainly didn't want her neighbors whispering about "Poor Missus Martin."

"I'm sorry? Were you addressing me?"

"Yes, ma'am. I don't see anyone else around here, do you?" He chuckled, and she wondered how he could laugh if he had just lost a loved one.

"Oh." She turned to go, but he reached out as if to touch her. "I really must be going. I'm sorry."

"Please, I really would like to know how people learn to cope with their loss. As I said, this is new to me."

"Um, who did you lose, if you don't mind my asking."

"My wife. We were traveling through here when she suddenly became very ill, and by the next morning she had passed. It was quite a shock. What about you?"

"My husband. It was also very sudden."

"How long has it been?"

Olivia was not sure she wanted to continue this conversation, but it was not in her nature to be rude. She felt sympathetic for this stranger, but she was also very uneasy. Something didn't feel right, so she carefully considered how much information she was willing to share.

"Not long, just a few months. Now if you'll excuse me, I must be getting home. I'm sorry for your loss," she quickly said, then turned to go. When she reached the street, she hurried toward town where she would feel a little safer having more people around. Something about that man unsettled her, but she wasn't sure exactly what it was.

As she neared her street, she quickly glanced over her shoulder to see if the stranger was following. Not seeing anyone, she felt herself relax a little, but a shiver ran down her spine. The whole encounter concerned her. She would need to keep herself extra vigilant in case he found out where she lived or attempted to harm one of the children. They had both been taught to be aware of their surroundings and to be cautious around strangers, but they were still young and would need to be reminded.

She hurried down the street to her house, the one Peter had built for them when they were first married fifteen years ago. Her mouth formed a sad smile as she remembered the excitement of creating a home and family with him. She had heard other women talking about how their husbands brought them to a house and expected them to accept it, but it had never been that way with her and Peter. He wanted her involved in every decision that was made as the house was built. They spent hours in the evenings talking about ideas they had to make it special, and the end result was something they both loved.

Olivia hustled into the kitchen to get dinner started so she would have time with the children when they arrived home from school. Her thoughts turned to the changes she had noticed in their behavior since Peter died. She knew she needed to increase her efforts to fill in the gap he had left, so she decided to make a batch of their favorite cookies for a special treat. It had been too long since she had the energy it required; they had all been just simply getting by on the basic meals she was able to prepare. At twelve, Frannie was developing her skills in the kitchen and was becoming a decent cook. Olivia was grateful, but her mothering instincts told her she should not depend on her child for so much.

The last batch of cookies had just come out of the oven and were cooling on the table when she heard two sets of footsteps on the front porch. She pasted on a smile that didn't quite reach her eyes and went to greet them just as the door swung open. "Hello, my darlings. Did you have a good day at school?"

Frannie pushed past her and ran up the stairs, while Michael came in for a hug. She glanced up the stairs after her daughter, concern etched on her face, but she spoke softly to her son. "Hey, buddy. Are you okay?"

Her ten year old son had grown up so much in the last few months that he had learned to sense her moods and anticipate concerned questions. "I guess so. Nothing happened, we just really miss Papa. I don't have anyone to play catch with me anymore, and Frannie won't play. That's why she's sad, because I asked her to. Then we talked about how we both miss him so much. He was going to build me that treehouse this spring. Now I guess I won't get to have one." With a deep sigh and slumped shoulders, he walked away from her.

"I'm sorry, son. I know you miss him every bit as much as I do. And I know it doesn't change anything, but I made your favorite cookies today. Why don't you wash your hands and have a few with a glass of milk while I go talk to your sister."

Michael grinned and darted into the kitchen. Olivia watched him go, relieved to realize that as painful as their loss was, kids were resilient, and eventually they would be okay. Probably sooner than she would. She turned and went upstairs to find Frannie.

"Hey, honey, may I come in?" Olivia knocked on the doorframe of her daughter's room. She was glad that Frannie had not closed the door, and she was able to see her slight nod. That was a good sign. At least she wasn't being metaphorically closed out, and she knew she would work hard to keep it that way. "What's on your mind, honey? Is there anything I can do to help?"

"I don't know. I'm just mad that Papa isn't here anymore." Tears formed in the corners of the girl's eyes, and Olivia struggled to keep her own tears at bay. This wasn't about her. This was pain her child was experiencing, and she wanted nothing more than to take it from her.

"Are you thinking of something specific that makes you sad? I know there doesn't have to be a special reason, and it's always okay to cry. Those are normal emotions when someone we love is gone."

The tears flowed as Frannie struggled to put her thoughts into words. Finally, she took a deep breath and, playing with her fingers on her lap, spoke. "We were making daisy chains outside after lunch today.

Some of the girls were talking about when we grow up and get married, how they want to put flowers in their hair. One girl talked about how her Papa would walk with her through the church and hand her off to her new husband." She rolled her eyes dramatically. "It's silly, I know, because that's forever away for us because we are only twelve, but then I got sad that my papa wouldn't be here to do that with me. Then I got mad because he left us like that. It just isn't fair!" She began sobbing, and Olivia gathered her into her arms and held her, her own tears flowing freely along with her daughter's.

"I know, darling, I know. It isn't fair at all. Many things in life are not fair. We have to learn to trust that God will take care of us and ease the pain. He will, as time goes on. Every day will get better. I know that doesn't fill the hole your papa left in our hearts, but he wouldn't want us to stay sad forever, either, right?" Olivia knew she was saying the right words, even if her heart didn't yet believe them.

Frannie nodded her head against her mother's shoulder. "I know. I'm just feeling sorry for myself right now. Maybe I just needed to cry. I'll be ok, Mama"

"That's my girl. You know you can always talk to me, right?"

"Yes, but I don't want to make you feel sadder. I think you are hurting more than I am with Papa being gone."

"Nothing you can do will make me feel sadder, darling. You talk to me about anything, anytime, okay? I want to know what you are feeling. It's my job as your mama to help you understand your feelings and to learn how to cope with things. Is there anything else you'd like to talk about?"

Frannie gave her mama a watery smile and hugged her. "No, but thank you, Mama. I'm glad you're still here. You're the best. I love you."

"I love you, too, sweetheart. Now, how about coming downstairs with me? I have a special surprise for you."

Chapter Four

Anticipation filled James as he pushed his horse to move a little faster. It was getting close to sunset, but he was almost home. He was eager to see the looks on his parent's faces when he walked through the door. He hoped he would arrive before dinner since he had only been nibbling on the dried meat and bread that Mrs. Fields had packed for him when he left Orchard Grove a few hours ago. He wondered what wonderful meal Cookie had prepared for them today. His mouth watered just thinking about her cooking.

To keep from obsessing about food, he turned his thoughts to the events of this morning. He and Matt had visited Gunther Schmidt's farm, wanting to speak with his sister. At first, Gretchen had refused to come out of the house. They explained their intention to Gunther, that they suspected that she had been unlawfully forced from her home and the same thing was happening to others around the area, and they wanted to put a stop to this criminal activity.

Finally, he convinced Gretchen to talk to them. She told them about a man wearing a dark coat and hat that came to her house and said that he could tell her home was in need of repairs. He could provide someone to do the work, and all it would cost her was room and board for the man. He tried to insist on her signing the papers right then, but she had refused, saying she wanted to look them over first. The man, who had been pleasant up to that point, became angry and said she was in violation of the town's ordinance, and that he would return the next day.

James remembers looking at Matt, both of them confused over what ordinance he could possibly be referring to since neither of them knew of such a thing, especially in the small mining towns. With the time allotted to him on his circuit, James had not visited all of them. People knew which of the larger towns he would be in as well as the approximate dates, so they could come to him whenever there was a matter that needed his attention.

Gretchen continued her story, telling them that he had indeed returned the next day with two additional men. They showed her a document that said she must leave within three days since she refused to comply with the ordinance. When they asked her what the original document said, she told them she hadn't had a chance to read it since he didn't leave it with her.

James' blood boiled at the thought that someone was driving innocent people out of their homes. It was nothing but a scare tactic, and women of all ages were being targeted simply because they were alone. He knew in his gut this was the same man who had been a guest of Mrs. Fields, and it made him wonder how many other widows were being affected. It also confirmed his suspicion that the man from the boarding house was not acting alone. What were they after?

It might make more sense if all the properties they were stealing - because, truthfully, that is exactly what was happening - were near a profitable mine or even in a location that had prime real estate. However, this was not the case. The targets seemed random and widespread. He wanted to find out what the motivation was. The sooner they had answers, the better. He wanted them stopped. He would be visiting the city soon and would call on his colleague to see if he had heard reports about this illegal activity. In spite of the towns adding extra deputies to help find these men, so far, they had not been caught.

    James turned his horse, Justice, into the lane leading to Jessup Plantation just as dusk settled across the fields. He rode slowly up the long lane that was lined with huge trees which formed a canopy over the path, and memories from his childhood came rushing in. The family's big, furry hound, Toby, ran to greet him, tongue lolling, yipping his welcome. Before he made it to the stables, his Pa came out onto the large porch that surrounded the house to see what the dog was barking about and was thrilled when he recognized his eldest son's figure climbing down off his horse.

"James! What a wonderful surprise, lad! I'm so pleased you're here! Your mother will be thrilled!"

Quickening his steps, he approached his father. "Pa! It's so good to see you! How have you been?"

"Better now you're here," Henry replied with a laugh as he hugged his son. The older man still spoke with the strong Scottish brogue of his homeland. "We've been just fine, just fine. Busy, of course, preparing for Emily Rose's wedding, but we canna complain. The Lord has given us good health and the strength to get it all done." He smiled, and James nodded, grateful that his parents were well. Being gone for so long at a time, he was never sure what to expect when he returned for a visit, but this time he was not leaving again, and he was glad how things were working out. He wanted to be close by to help if needed, and to spend more of whatever time they had left on this earth with them.

Henry called out to one of the youngsters who worked in the stables to come take Justice so that James could come inside to see his mother. He followed his father into the house to the kitchen, and his mother nearly dropped the plate she was holding when she saw him.

"James! Oh, James! I can't believe you are here already! Oh, I'm so happy!! Come here and let me hug you!"

Laughing, James willingly complied. "Hello, Mama. How are you?"

"Just wonderful! Are you hungry? We are just ready to sit down for dinner. Cookie, we need another plate!

Soon, Mama was ushering them to the dining room as Emily Rose came from the library, a tall young man trailing her. When she saw him, she squealed and, though it was unladylike, ran and jumped into his waiting arms. "James!! I can't believe you are here! Oh, come here, you have to meet Jacob!"

Laughing, James turned to greet the young man who would soon be marrying his youngest sister. "James, this," she paused with a dreamy look on her face, "is Jacob Smyth. Jacob, my big brother, James."

She squealed again and clapped her hands. Everyone laughed at her antics. She was still a little bit dramatic, as she always had been, but they all adored her, so it was overlooked since she was the baby of the family.

"Jacob, it's good to finally meet you.

"Wonderful to meet you as well, sir," Jacob replied as they shook hands. Emily Rose giggled at the notion of someone calling her brother "sir".

Catherine spoke up, urging them to find their seats at the table. "Come on, everyone. Please sit so we can eat before the food is cold, then James can tell us everything. Would you bless the meal, James?"

After the food was served and the first pangs of hunger had been chased away, everyone started asking questions, and James told them as much as he could about life on the road. He told stories about heartbreak, and stories that had them laughing. Lastly, he told them about the trouble he had recently encountered and how Gretchen and Mrs. Fields had been threatened. He mentioned his intention of meeting with a colleague in Greensboro to see if he could learn more about this group of "property bandits" as he had begun calling them in his mind.

"Is that why you're home sooner than we expected you, Son?" Catherine asked. "So that you can do that before returning to the circuit after the wedding?

James smiled, then looked around the table at each person, and returned his gaze to his mother. "Actually, there is more to the story. I refrained from talking about it to anyone until we knew for sure things would work out, but I found someone to cover the circuit courts for me. Permanently."

Catherine gasped, and Henry leaned back in his chair, a sheen coming to his eyes. True to form, Emily Rose squealed and clapped. Catherine spoke first. "How did this all come about?"

Grinning, James told how he had been getting restless for the last couple of years, and the last time he was home, he contacted his mentor, asking if he knew of a young judge who would perhaps be interested in the role. He told how he had met Roger Jefferies and had a very good first impression, and that they had done the circuit together for several months, and Roger was now ready to be on his own.

"What does that mean for you, now?" Henry asked.

"I will be staying around here. I hope you all don't mind," he grinned. "I want to start a private practice again here in Jessup. It's time to come home."

"I can't think of anything that would make us happier than to have you home for good, James. That's the best news I've heard in a while," his mother said with tears in her eyes. "Of course, you can stay here for as long as you like. I know you're used to having your own space, but you are welcome here. Especially since Emily Rose will soon be leaving. I'm not ready for the house to be so empty."

Chuckling, James said, "Mama, my 'own space', as you call it, is on the back of my horse, camping on the ground and hoping it doesn't rain, or staying in one of several boarding houses. I'd be happy to stay here in one place for a while until I find a place to set up my office in town. Then, maybe I'll find a place to live there. Either way, you will be seeing a lot more of me from now on."

Conversation eventually turned to other things. James caught up on a lot of the family gossip and was delighted to get to know Jacob. There was teasing and laughter, and above all, there was a lot of love. He couldn't wait to see the rest of his siblings. They all had homes of their own now. How strange that notion was. Soon, he would be the only one without a family of his own. He refused to let those melancholy thoughts linger right now. He would have time later to think about Victoria and John when he wasn't visiting with his parents and sister.

As they all rose from the table, he said, "Mama, as always, that was a wonderful meal. Thank you." And he gave her another hug.

"You don't have to thank me, but I appreciate it. You know Cookie does most of the work in the kitchen." She hugged him back and held on a little longer than usual. "I'm so happy you're home to stay!"

"So am I, Mama. It was time."

They moved out onto the veranda with cups of coffee. The evening was very pleasant, promising sun and warmth for the next day. They enjoyed another hour of conversation before Jacob took his leave, assuring Emily Rose he would return the next day. After he left, they all went their separate ways, retiring to their rooms for the night.

James sighed, content to be in familiar surroundings with his family nearby. Now he could relax and let the memories flow over him. Occasionally, they still leaked out his eyes and ran down his cheeks, but he refused to allow that to happen in his family's presence. He didn't want to make them worry about him. He was fine. In fact, he had been wondering if it was time to open himself up to finding another wife, someone to share the rest of his life with. Maybe that was the missing piece in his life.

Before crawling into his bed, he knelt to pray. *"Lord, thank you for bringing me safely home. Thank you for Roger being willing to take over the circuit. Thank you for allowing me all those years of helping so many people. Guide my steps now as I seek to start something new here. And Lord, if it's in your will, I'm ready for you to give me another woman to love and care for, someone who will fill my days with whatever it is I've been missing. Amen."*

Chapter Five

Two days later, James rode into Greensboro to visit his mentor and friend, Judge Nathan Gray. He walked up the wide, long marble staircase of the stately looking county courthouse and made his way around the side hall to Nathan's office. Stepping inside, he was greeted by the smiling, wrinkled face of Mrs. Gray, Nathan's wife and secretary.

Coming around her reception desk, she reached out to pull him in for a warm, motherly hug. "James! How good it is to see you! What brings you all the way to the city?"

Smiling and returning the hug, he said, "Hello, Mrs. Gray. It's good to see you, also! I came to see if Nathan is available for a chat."

"He should be in just a few moments. He's finishing up with a client right now. Would you like something to drink? Please, have a seat and tell me what's been going on in your life. How are things up in the mountains?"

Chuckling, James accepted a glass of water from her and briefly described some of his work while he waited for Nathan. He was careful to avoid talking about the trouble that had been brewing in the mining towns, and instead regaled her with a few of the funnier anecdotes and charming stories of real people in the outlying areas. He updated her on his family, telling her about the upcoming wedding of his sister, Emily Rose. Just as Nathan opened the door to walk his client out, she told him to extend her congratulations to his sister.

Nathan's greeting was just as warm as his wife's. There was a merry twinkle in the older gentleman's eyes that made him seem more approachable than some judges James had met. A few minutes later, Nathan invited him into his office, and they sat down to talk. James told him about introducing Roger to the circuit over the past several months, and how well that seemed to be going. He thanked him again for putting him in contact with Roger and commended him for his ability to read people so well. He also told him his plans to open an office in Jessup and plant roots there.

After getting caught up on each other's lives, Nathan asked, "So, why are you really here? What's going on up there?"

"Have you heard of any ordinances in the small towns requiring a certain standard of upkeep on homes?"

Nathan raised his eyebrows, then frowned in thought. "As far as I know there is no such thing. Because those areas are under this county's jurisdiction, such laws would have to pass through my office. I have not even seen any proposals for such an ordinance. These "property bandits", as you so aptly call them, are completely out of line. Let's just hope there are not many of them operating."

"That's what I thought, and that's why I came here first. I wanted to make sure it wasn't something new that I missed hearing about while I was up there. Whispers of trouble started coming my way up in the mining camps, but it has trickled out as far as Orchard Grove. I stopped at Mrs. Fields's boarding house on my way home, and she, too, has been approached by a sharply dressed gentleman, offering to have her place brought up to their standards in exchange for room and board for the worker. And her place looks a lot nicer than some of the places both in and out of town."

"I wonder what their catch is. They certainly are not offering help out of the goodness of their hearts. There must be more to it."

"Yes, there is. Gretchen said the man who threatened her refused to allow her the chance to read the documents he wanted her to sign, and she was terrified, so she just left and went to her brother for protection. Mrs. Fields, on the other hand, is more spunky." James chuckled. "She took the papers and refused to give them back, asking how she would know if she wanted to sign them unless she could read them first. She gave them to me, and both Matt and I read them. It's not good. Buried in the middle of the last page is a paragraph stating that the property would be turned over to them should the owner abandon the premises. Somehow, these bandits have created a document which supposedly legalizes theft of homes. As far as I can see, they are persuading these lonely widows to have unnecessary work done by a stranger who was to live in their home. What woman would agree to that? Instead, they flee out of fear and give up everything their husband worked for. We have to find these men and stop them."

"And then, most likely, they would sell the property to someone else. That's their motivation."

"I agree. That's what I think too. Matt and I discussed it at length, and I told him to start putting his deputies on watch for newly widowed women. I think that's why they are being targeted. They are grieving and unsure of what the law says, so this group is taking advantage of them."

Nathan stroked his chin and nodded. "It wouldn't be a bad idea to post a watch all over the county. I'll send out a notice to surrounding county judges as well, letting them know what we have going on and what our suspicions are. Meanwhile, if you will send telegrams to Roger and all the sheriffs and marshals in the circuit, maybe we can get this stopped."

"I certainly will, before I leave town today. Thank you, Nathan. And tomorrow I will start looking for a place to set up my new office. I want to be available should any of them need me. It was great to see you again! I'll leave you to get back to your busy schedule."

"Thanks for coming in, James. Keep me informed on this, will you?"

"Of course! See you soon, my friend."

The two men shook hands, and James left the courthouse. He headed for the telegraph office, drafting his message in his mind as he went.

***

The following day, James went into the town of Jessup to find space for his law office. While he had been on the circuit, he had learned that the practice he was once part of had moved to the city, leaving the residents in rural Guilford County with no one to help with their legal needs. He was excited and anxious to get set up and provide these good people with his services.

On the edge of town was the pretty little cemetery where he had buried his beloved wife and son so many years before. He slowed his horse, then on a whim, turned in and dismounted, tying Justice to the rail near the gate. Looking around, he was amazed at how many more graves there were. Most looked several years old, but a few looked much newer as the ground had not completely settled. After a moment, he walked to the familiar location and squatted down, brushing the old leaves and debris from the stone.

"Hello, my darling. I'm sorry it's been so long since I came for a visit. I just wanted to tell you that I decided I've been running for far too long and it's time to come home. My family is overjoyed, as I knew they would be, but this part, being back in town and setting up a law practice again, will be hard without you here.

I miss you so much, every day. I never knew what pain was until I lost you. God has been good, though. He has taught me so much about living that I thought I already knew. He taught me that He is more than enough to sustain me, but it took me a while to learn that one. One of the advantages of living life on the circuit was all the time in the saddle. I either had to talk to myself or to God, and He has more answers than I do." James smiled. *"Anyway, I'm okay. I'm in a good place mentally and emotionally, and I'm ready to plant roots and help the good people of our hometown again."*

James remained quiet for a few moments as memories flowed over him: her smile, her laugh, how she felt in his arms, the way she teased him that made him laugh, and especially how happy she was anticipating the birth of their baby. He swiped at a stray tear as he recalled that day, cradling his son who never took his first breath, then placing him in her arms before she became too weak and lifeless. He remembered working silently alongside Pa as they went about the terrible task of building the caskets. His pa was a great source of strength for him during that time. He didn't say much. He hadn't needed to. James would always be grateful for him, especially during the most difficult days of his life.

He rose to his full height then and said a prayer, thanking God for allowing him to grow and learn from his experience, making him a better man because of it. He asked again for wisdom in finding just the right place for his office and requesting that the people be directed to him at the right time. He asked for wisdom to serve the people of this town and the surrounding area. And he asked God to help the deputies of the county track down the men responsible for tormenting the women who, through no fault of their own, were left defenseless, so that they may be brought to justice through the law.

James swung back into the saddle and rode on into town slowly, looking around at all the changes that had taken place over the years. Soon, he reached the street where he and Victoria had lived. Their house sat on the corner of Main Street and Maple. It was a striking structure, elegant looking, made of dark red brick and trimmed in white. It had two stories, with large windows in the front parlor overlooking a wide porch. He remembered the day he finished the pair of rocking chairs he had made for them so that they could sit on the porch and watch people walk by.

As he got closer, he realized that the garden was overgrown, and some paint was chipping. The small carriage house in the back was in disrepair and the door was hanging haphazardly on a hinge. Concerned that this place could be targeted by the property bandits, he dismounted, tied Justice to a branch, and went up on the porch to knock on the door.

It did not take long for James to realize no one was around, so he boldly looked in the front window. What he saw should not have shocked him, considering the way the outside of the house appeared. The sparse furnishings that remained were damaged and dirty, and it was evident that animals had been nesting inside.

James strode back down the steps, remounted Justice, and rode on into town in search of the sheriff.

He wanted to know what had happened to the previous tenants. He quickly moved through town to his destination and stopped near a watering trough to let Justice have a drink before tying him to the rail. Then, stepping into the sheriff's office, he removed his hat and met the other man's eyes.

"How can I help you, sir?" Sheriff Ben Richardson was a few years younger than James, tall and lanky, but carried an air of someone who didn't tolerate nonsense.

"Good morning, sir. I'm James MacKay, come to make your acquaintance."

"Ah! The circuit judge. I've heard about you! I'm Ben Richardson," he said, reaching out for a handshake.

James chuckled, accepting the hand. "I hope that's not a bad thing."

Ben laughed. "Not at all. I hear you are a wise and fair judge."

"Thank you. I appreciate hearing that."

"What can I do for you, James?"

"Well, I'm wondering what you can tell me about a vacant house a few blocks down, corner of Main and Maple." James watched the other man's face. He had learned that people tell a lot with their expressions when taken off guard. He wasn't disappointed, but what he saw was sadness.

"Sad story. The family who lived there were all killed in a carriage accident last fall. Good people. Loved by everyone. Father, mother, and several children. Horse mis stepped and went off the bridge, taking the whole family with them. It was the worst loss this area has seen in a while. We sure do miss that family around here." Ben shook his head, staring unfocused into the distance.

"Wow, I'm really sorry to hear about that. But, what about the property? Was there no one to claim it?"

"Nah, there was no mortgage, so the bank had no claim on it. There was no extended family that we could find. Now that warm weather is here, we'll need to do something about it, but no one has stepped up to do that yet. Any particular reason you're asking?

"As a matter of fact, yes. I would be interested in claiming it. I'm looking for a place to establish a law practice here in town, and I think that would be a good location."

"So, you're hanging up your judge's robe?"

James laughed. "Not entirely, but I'm done being on the circuit and ready to plant roots again."

"You're from around here, aren't you?"

"Yes. I grew up at Jessup Plantation and lived here for a short time before my wife died."

"Oh, I'm sorry to hear that. If you're serious about that place, let's go over to the land office and see what you'll need to do to take ownership. It will be good to have another law office in town. The last one left a couple of years ago, and it's been tough having to go all the way to Greensboro when we need something done. Come on. The land office is just down the block."

Chapter Six

Olivia washed her hands after setting a batch of bread to rise. She was determined to bring things in the house back to normal, if not for her own sake, then for the sake of the children. They deserved all the care she used to put into keeping their home neat and tidy, and little details she put into each of their family meals. Baking fresh bread today was a step in that direction. Next, she would wash and hang the bedding, freshen it up and give it that good, clean air smell.

Just as she was heading upstairs, there was a knock at the door. She frowned, wondering who it could be. It had been months since she'd had any visitors, so she made her way to the front of the house and opened the door. A tall, fair-haired man in a dark coat smiled and doffed his hat.

"Good morning, ma'am. I'm looking for the man of the house. Is he by chance home today?"

Olivia was thrown off her mental balance momentarily, but quickly gathered her wits to respond. Careful not to give too much information, she replied, "No, I'm sorry, he is not. Is there something I can help you with?"

"I really need to speak to him. This is a matter of utmost importance."

"I'm sorry, but that won't be possible. What is this all about?"

The man's eyes darkened a bit, and he pulled some papers out of the inside pocket of his coat. "It has come to our attention that there are some repairs that must be done on your house. You are in violation of the ordinance requiring each home to maintain certain standards of care. Now, we have a man who will be happy to come take care of the required changes. It won't cost you anything for the labor, just give him room and board while the work is being done. I'm sure there are things inside that need attention also. Just sign these papers and we'll have you in compliance very soon."

She reached out to take the papers. "I'll need to read this before I agree to sign it. Please give me some time." She took a step back to close the door, but his foot got in the way, keeping the door open. Olivia's eyes went wide, and she felt panic rise up, trying to choke her. What was happening? Who was he and why had she never heard of such an ordinance? Peter had kept the house in good repair, and she was not aware of anything that needed fixing, so this did not settle well with her at all.

"Sir, please remove your foot from my doorway and leave my property immediately!" She tried pushing the door again, and rather than create a scene with the neighbors, he shifted his foot back, but as he did so, he grabbed the papers out of her hand before she slammed the door and locked it. Olivia shook as she went to the front room and peeked through the window, watching the man walk away. Just as he got to the street, he turned and gave the house a menacing look.

Olivia sat down abruptly. That was terrifying! What was the meaning of this? She wished there was someone she could talk to about it, someone who could help her understand the laws and whether or not her home was in some sort of violation. Suddenly, it occurred to her that a new law firm had opened just down the street, and the name seemed familiar. Maybe this was someone she could trust to give her good legal advice. After checking to be sure the man was truly gone, she grabbed her shawl and went out the door.

***

James was on a ladder, working to rehang the door to the carriage house when his eye caught movement behind him. Turning slightly, he watched as a woman stopped at the end of his sidewalk. She was looking at the sign he had hung two days ago announcing the opening of his law practice, 'James MacKay, Attorney at Law'. She seemed to be debating going to the house.

The past week had been pretty busy as he took possession of the house that had once belonged to him and Victoria. His mother and sisters came to help, and had cleaned it from top to bottom until not even a particle of dust could be found in the corners. The wood and windows sparkled and gleamed. His brothers came when they were able to spare a few hours, and now all the first floor interior walls sported new paint. The downstairs was finally restored to its former beauty.

He was grateful there was no serious damage; it only needed some loving care. Repairs to the outside were more significant, but still not terrible. He had seen many places in a lot worse condition after being abandoned. It was evident that the former owners, the family he had sold his home to all those years ago, had taken as much pride in it as he had, and he was appreciative.

He climbed down from the ladder and walked toward the woman. "Hello! I'm James MacKay. How can I help you?"

She seemed startled when he spoke, like she didn't realize anyone was around. She stared at him for a moment, then frowned briefly before answering quietly. "Hello. I'm Olivia Martin, but I'm not sure if you can help me."

"Would you like to come inside? Tell me what's going on and I'll tell you whether or not I can help."

She hesitated, a look of fear causing shadows to run across her face. James waited for her response, but in that moment, he knew something or someone was causing her to be afraid, and for reasons he didn't understand, he wanted to wipe the worry from her mind and protect her. He extended a hand toward the front porch, indicating she should join him, and quickly changed his approach.

"It's such a nice day, how about if we sit on the porch. I'll go get us a refreshing drink. Is that alright with you?"

Olivia smiled slightly, sadness dimming her pretty blue eyes. "Yes, the porch sounds nice. It looks so inviting."

"Thank you. That was my intention." James smiled and allowed her to go ahead of him up the walkway to the steps. After she was seated, he went inside to get them each a glass of sweetened cold tea. He sat down in a chair far enough away not to frighten her, but close enough that their conversation could be quiet. He recognized her reticence and wanted to make sure she felt safe in talking to him.

After a few moments, Olivia glanced up at him. "Thank you. I wasn't sure who I could talk to, but something has happened that has caused me to feel alarmed." She was obviously nervous and upset. James could see the liquid in the glass quivering as her hands shook slightly.

Quietly, he said, "If it helps, let me tell you a little of my background, then you can decide if you want to trust me. Would that be okay?"

She nodded, a grateful look softening her face. "I grew up near here, so anyone who lives around here knows my family. For the last fifteen years, I have been a circuit judge to the west of here in small towns and up into the mountains. My friend and mentor, Judge Nathan Gray in Greensboro, would vouch for me, as would any of the marshals, sheriffs, and deputies in the county. In fact, if your troubles are such that the sheriff needs to be involved, I'd be happy to have Ben Richardson come by, or we could go to him."

Olivia inhaled quickly, fear showing on her face again as she shook her head. "No, I would rather not do that, at least not yet. However, I am afraid that what I have to say needs to be told, so I'm going to have to just trust you right now."

"Alright. Go ahead, whenever you're ready. There's no rush." He sat back in his chair in a patient and relaxed posture. He had learned over his years in this business that people will talk more easily if the atmosphere is calm. They sat in silence for a few more minutes, then the story started pouring out.

"My husband died from an injury a few months ago. He was trying to get a roof finished on a house he and his team were building. It was rainy that day, and they were hurrying to finish before the next storm came through. It started to rain, but he only had a few more shingles to nail down, so instead of coming down, he kept working. Just as he completed the last one, his foot slipped on the wet shingles, and he fell to the ground. The fall broke his back, and the doctor said some ribs punctured his lungs. There was nothing anyone could do." As her voice trailed off, tears that she was so bravely trying to keep back broke through the dam and spilled down her face.

James reached into his pocket and handed her his handkerchief. "I'm so sorry, Missus Martin." She took it silently and wiped her face, trying to dry all the tears that refused to stop flowing. Eventually, she took a deep, shaky breath and slowly blew it out.

Olivia looked up at James, sorrow in her features. "I'm sorry I broke down like that. I should not have allowed that to happen."

"You don't ever need to apologize for grieving. It's still so fresh and raw, you need to give it time. Eventually it won't hurt quite so much."

"It almost seems like you know that from experience."

"I do." James hesitated. How much should he reveal to this woman who was obviously so torn up over the loss of her husband? Would sharing his story help or make her hurt even worse? Making his decision, he plunged ahead.

"Fifteen years ago, my wife and I were living here, in this very house. I was practicing law with a partner here in town, and we were thrilled to be expecting our first child. Life was wonderful. When the time came for the baby to be born, there were…," he hesitated, swallowing hard, "…complications. Our son was born, but he never took his first breath. Victoria was weak; she had lost a lot of blood. I sensed that the doctor was very concerned, so I wrapped our son and placed him in her arms. She held him close and kissed his soft hair, tears streaming down her face as the life drained out of her." He stopped, unaware that a single tear was making its way down his cheek.

In telling his story, even after all this time, he was transported back fifteen years as vividly as if it had happened yesterday. Perhaps it was being back in this house again. Maybe this had not been such a good idea after all. Suddenly he was aware there was a warm hand on his arm. He looked down, realizing that Olivia was crouching near him, her hand touching him in a comforting gesture. "I'm so sorry, Mister MacKay. I know how devastating that must have been for you."

James cleared his throat, his voice raspy when he spoke again. "I'm sorry. You came here to ask for help, and here I am pouring my heart out to you. That was unprofessional. Please forgive me."

"No forgiveness is necessary. I can tell you are still missing them, and that helps me feel better about my own loss. And it encourages me that I can trust you, so thank you for showing me that side of you."

Olivia stood and walked to the railing at the edge of the porch, looking into the distance. "Would you like more tea, Missus Martin?"

Turning back toward him, she smiled slightly and shook her head. "No, but thank you. I would like to tell you why I came here today, if you don't mind."

"Of course! Please continue."

"A few days ago, I was in the cemetery having a talk with Peter, and when I was leaving, a man approached me. He asked if it was my husband who had died. It made me uncomfortable, and I wasn't sure what or how much to say, so I asked him who he had lost. He claimed to have just lost his wife after a sudden illness as they were traveling through this area, but I felt suspicious as I hadn't noticed any fresh graves. I reluctantly told him yes, it was my husband that had died. He wanted to know how long ago, saying he wanted to know how other people cope with their loss. I told him it had just been a few months, then excused myself and went home, making sure he wasn't following me. I didn't think any more about it other than to remind my children to be vigilant and not talk to strangers, particularly men."

She paused as though gathering her thoughts. James remained quiet, absorbing the information even as his mind raced, wondering if there was any connection to the so-called property bandits. While he waited for her to continue, she began pacing back and forth in front of him.

"This morning, there was a knock on my door. A well-dressed gentleman in a long, dark coat requested to speak to my husband. I told him that would not be possible and asked what it was regarding. He became gruff and said that my home was in disrepair and in violation of some ordinance. He handed me some papers and told me to sign them. The repairs would not cost me anything but room and board for the man doing the work. I was in shock, because Peter kept our home in good condition. I know of nothing that needs repair!"

James shot to his feet, running a hand through his hair. "Please describe this man, and the one who approached you in the cemetery. They were not the same person, is that correct?"

"Yes, that is correct. The man in the cemetery was well-dressed, I would say less than six feet tall, dark brown hair and maybe brown eyes, but I'm not sure. He was wearing a long, dark coat. The man today was tall, thin, with blond hair and blue eyes that looked mean when I questioned him. His smile never met his eyes."

"Thank you. What else did he say to you?" James watched her intently as she continued.

"I told him I would read them over before signing anything, and when I started to close the door, he put his foot in the way. I was terrified! I pulled strength from somewhere and told him to move his foot. After what seemed like several moments, he finally did, but just before the door closed, he reached out and grabbed the papers back from me. I locked the door and watched to be sure he left my property, but he gave a menacing look as he strode away."

By the time she finished her story, her chin was quivering, and her voice wavered. The reaction that surfaced surprised James: he wanted to gather her in his arms and comfort her. Abruptly, he sat back down, distancing himself and working to get his thoughts in check. Olivia moved to the chair she had previously occupied and sat down as well. Gradually, James was aware that she was watching him, presumably waiting for a response. He scrambled to school his features. He did not want to frighten her, but he did want to reassure her that he would try to help.

Releasing a breath he didn't realize he was holding, he met her gaze. "I am so sorry this is happening to you, but I am glad you came to me with your story. As a matter of fact, we have been searching for a group of men, we don't know how many, who have been trying to swindle widows out of their property." Olivia gasped, her jaw dropping. "We started hearing similar stories in the mountains, primarily in mining towns, and a few other stories in the foothills. These men are getting bolder, but we don't know exactly what their motives are. Whatever you do, do not sign anything without checking with me first, and do not let anyone into your home that you don't know. I think what they are doing is gaining entry by the man they claim will be doing the "work", and somehow forcing the women out using scare tactics. Once the property is abandoned, they take ownership. So far, I only know of one woman who held her ground, so I'm not sure what lengths the men will go to to get possession of the property. You just stand strong, okay?"

Olivia's wide eyes met his as he spoke. He didn't want to scare her, but he wanted her to understand how serious this was. This might be a good way to capture these men, and he was glad he would be close enough to help do that. He would be sure and tell Ben what had happened, also. These criminals must be caught, and it must happen soon. Enough was enough!

"I need to notify Ben of what happened. Is that okay with you?" She nodded. "Would you like to come with me to do that?"

"No, I want to go back home. My children will be coming back from school soon and I don't want them to be there alone."

"That is understandable. May I ask where you live? I want to provide you with some protection without alerting the whole neighborhood." He smiled at her look of surprise.

"My home is just down this street, the fourth house on the right."

James filed that information away for later. Memories were swirling around in his mind of things from years before. He didn't want to examine those thoughts just yet, not while Missus Martin was still on his porch. There would be plenty of time for that later.

"May I walk back with you, to make sure no one is lurking around?"

Surprise registered on Olivia's face as she paused briefly. "I would appreciate that. Thank you, Mister MacKay."

"Since we are neighbors, why don't you call me James," he said with a grin.

Bashfully, she smiled. "Then you must call me Olivia."

Chapter Seven

What had gotten into him? James told himself he was simply being neighborly in offering to walk with Olivia back to her home. Besides, wasn't it part of his job to help find and prosecute these bandits who had tried to steal her home from her? He was only protecting an innocent woman, right? James pushed these thoughts out of his mind. He would be able to examine them more closely later. Meanwhile, he should find out more about her and her family.

"Tell me about your children," he said to make her comfortable carrying on conversation as they walked.

"I have two. My daughter, Francine, but we call her Frannie, is a precocious twelve year old, and my son, Michael, is a sweet and lovable ten year old."

"And how are they handling their father being gone?" James asked softly.

"They have occasional outbursts, but mostly they have tried to take care of me. I feel terrible about that. I allowed my sorrow to steal some of their childhood, but now I am trying to keep things as normal as I can."

"I'm sure it is very difficult for all of you, but you have to remember, they are not the only ones who lost someone. You did, too. On top of that, you are suddenly thrust into the role of both mother and father, and they suddenly only have one parent. You should give yourself some grace. It seems to me if they are trying to take care of you, you did a remarkable job of raising them to be loving and kind."

Olivia contemplated his assessment, then tilted her head, looking up at him. "Thank you for those encouraging words. You don't know how much I needed to hear them. My husband always affirmed me, even when I doubted myself. He never let me stay that way. He always told me to stop beating myself up. It's funny how, even now, I hear his voice in my head, reminding me."

"Did you say your husband's name was Peter?"

"Yes."

James stroked his chin thoughtfully. "I believe I knew him, many years ago. Earlier when you said his name, I thought it sounded familiar and I have been trying to place him. He was a few years younger than me, and if I recall, was friends with my brother, Edward."

Olivia's eyes brightened in recognition. "Yes! Edward MacKay! Now I know why your name seemed familiar, but with everything that has happened in recent weeks and months, I didn't put it together. He was a good friend to Peter for many years. Edward came by to check on us a few times after Peter's death. I appreciate his and Jenny's friendship, and our children are friends, too."

James laughed. "Isn't it amazing how things work out." They had reached her house, and James looked around. His eyes scanned the front of the structure, checking to see if anything seemed out of order. "How long have you lived here?"

"Fifteen years. Peter built it for us when we were first married."

"I thought as much. I seem to remember this house under construction just before Victoria died. If things were different, the two of you could have been friends."

"I'm sure I would have enjoyed that."

James and Olivia walked around the perimeter of the house while he looked for signs of an intruder under the guise of checking for things that needed repair. Except for a few branches on the big oak tree behind the house that needed to be cut off before they began scratching the windows, he didn't notice anything that needed attention. He made a mental note to come back with a saw and take care of those branches before they caused any damage.

***

James said farewell to Olivia and went into town to see Ben Richardson. He had a hard time keeping his anger reined in. What were these men thinking, preying on grieving widows like this? He was glad he had mentioned to a few sheriff friends to watch out for new graves. The information he had gotten from Olivia could be valuable, and if the bandits followed the same method of operation they seemed to have in the past, they would be returning to Olivia's house, and he intended to be nearby when it happened.

Walking into Ben's office, he greeted the other man with a handshake.

"Hello, there, Judge. What brings you here today?"

"Well, I'm afraid there is a situation."

"Nothing about the house, I hope?"

"No, everything is fine there. My family came and helped get the inside cleaned up so I could get the office opened, and I've been slowly getting the outside squared away so I can start on the living quarters."

"I saw you hung your sign, so I guess that means you're open for business."

"Yes, I am. It appears we will be working together now. At least we're on the same side of the law," James commented with a chuckle.

Ben laughed. "Absolutely! So, what's going on?"

James took a deep breath and began. "A few months ago, we learned of a group of men, we don't know how many, approaching people who had just lost a loved one. So far, it seems they are targeting women whose husbands have just passed, claiming they are in violation of some ordinance that doesn't exist within the law. They show a packet of documents, saying they need a signature, and a man will come do the required work in exchange for room and board."

Ben's eyes widened and he scratched his head. "What in the world! Are they getting away with it?"

"So far, they have, except in one case. A dear, elderly woman who runs a boarding house I stayed at in my rounds, refused to sign and did not give back the papers." James chuckled. "She's a spunky one. Five foot nothing, but no one crosses Missus Fields and gets away with it. She probably chased him off with a butcher knife!" The two men laughed at the mental picture his words conjured. "She let me and Matt O'Connor, the local sheriff there, examine the documents, and buried in the last page was a paragraph saying that if the owner abandoned the home, this group would take ownership."

Ben let out a low whistle and his fists clenched. "The audacity! How many folks have fallen prey to this scheme, I wonder?"

"We don't know for sure. We have no idea yet what their plan is once they take possession of the properties. Except for Missus Fields, it appears others have been frightened and ran off. Another young woman fled to her brother's home in Orchard Grove, and Matt and I were able to interview her."

"Wouldn't a land transfer have to pass through the courts? Or you, since they would have been within your circuit? It just don't make sense." Ben frowned, shaking his head.

"To make it legal, yes. We'll get the word out to law enforcement in those areas after we catch the culprits, any new residents will have to be screened to be sure they are on the land legally."

"What about having deputies visit newly widowed ladies and warn them?"

"We have, but by the time we have word of a death, it's already too late and the property is vacated."

Ben nodded thoughtfully. "So, what can I do to help?"

"This morning, a woman who lives just down the street from me came by, nervous as a long-tailed cat near a rocking chair. She told me how her husband died just a few months ago. She said she was approached in the cemetery a few days ago by a gentleman in a long dark coat, claiming to have lost his wife and asked her who she lost and how long ago. She felt unnerved, like something didn't settle quite right. This morning, a different man, also wearing a long dark coat, came to her door asking to speak to her husband. She said he wasn't available, and the man proceeded to bring out papers, saying her home was in violation of some ordinance. When she told him to leave, he tried to keep her from closing the door with his foot, but," James smirked, liking the strength she had demonstrated, "I think she used her 'mama' voice, telling him to move his foot. He finally did, but just before she slammed the door, he reached in and grabbed the papers from her. She said she watched to be sure he left, and he gave a menacing look toward the house. She was so frightened, she came to talk to me, hoping to find someone she could trust. Turns out, her husband and my brother, Edward, are - er, were - good friends."

"Wow. I cannot believe these men are terrorizing women. I don't have a wife, but I have a mother and sisters, and if that happened to them, I would be furious."

"I feel the same way. Like I said, I'm not sure what the motive is. All the properties are scattered at random. There doesn't seem to be a pattern. If there was, they would be pressuring more than just single women."

"Yes, it does seem so. This woman, is that Missus Martin?"

"Yes, it is."

"I thought so. She's a sweet woman. Peter's death was such a tragedy; it really shook the community. He was such a hard worker, and he employed a good sized crew of construction workers. Their reputation is quite good, known for good quality and integrity. Thankfully, a couple of the guys picked up the mantle and kept the business running. They even set up a fund for Peter's family to live on from the proceeds of the business. And the whole town turned out for his funeral. A devastating loss, that one. I'm glad she came to you for help."

"It seemed like she wasn't sure if she should talk to someone, and it took a little time to convince her I was safe." Ben grinned at James. "What?"

"She's a pretty lady." James couldn't deny that. "When people hear of your reputation, you'll be so busy you'll need to hire help. Maybe you need an assistant!" Ben waggled his eyebrows, teasing James.

James shook his head, grinning. "Let's not get ahead of ourselves, here. Let's just get these property bandits caught and put behind bars."

"Well, you never know who will cross your path in this life."

"For now, I just want to make sure she and her children are safe. And as much as I hate the idea, she may end up being the bait we need to catch them. When she went home, I walked with her and checked around the perimeter of the house. I couldn't find a single thing wrong that required fixing, even if it was a legitimate ordinance. Peter has done an outstanding job of taking care of their home." He didn't bother to mention his intention to take care of the branches on the tree behind her house. It might give Ben ammunition for more teasing. No, he needed to be professional, but there was no reason he couldn't be neighborly as well.

"I have a few men who are deputized to help me sometimes. I'll call them in and apprise them of this situation. I can have her house watched around the clock for a few days. We'll catch these guys and put them out of business."

"That sounds good. Can you put me on your list?"

Ben thought about it for a moment. "I'd like you to be here for the meeting. The men need to know who you are and that you are on our side. Depending on how many are available will determine whether we need you to watch. You might serve us better in another way. Can you be here tonight at eight o'clock?"

"I'll be here. Thanks, Ben."

"Thanks for bringing this to my attention, James. We'll find these creeps. Don't worry."

James walked back home, his mind tossing around possible reasons this group had for terrorizing widows. He hoped that the plan Ben came up with would solve the problem once and for all. He stopped by the telegraph office to send wires to both Matt O'Connor in Orchard Grove, and Nathan Gray in Greensboro, promising to keep them informed.

Chapter Eight

James finished hanging the door on the carriage house that he had been working on that morning, then put the ladder and tools inside. It was well past time he should have gone to the plantation, but because of the meeting with the sheriff and deputies in just a couple of hours, he chose instead to find something to eat here and work on a few other things in the office.

When he designed this house all those years ago, who would have ever guessed the downstairs would eventually be transformed into office space. What had once been the drawing room had easily morphed into his private office. One wall was lined with bookshelves that he was gradually filling with his law books from his parent's house, as well as a lot of other books for his reading pleasure. There was still a lot of empty space, but knowing his love for knowledge and entertainment, he had no doubt those vacancies would soon evaporate.

In the center of the room sat a large oak desk. His father's friend, Harley, had built it for him when he finished law school, but with things being as they were, it had remained at the plantation all these years. He was happy to be putting it to good use now. Around the desk, which also functioned as a table when clients came in, were several upholstered chairs in shades of brown and burgundy. They were comfortable and made his clients feel welcome. In the corner, opposite the window, stood a cabinet for keeping client files locked away from prying eyes.

The main room, which opened from the front porch of the house, had once been their parlor. The focal point at the center of the room was a large fireplace, with flat stones lining the walls around it. A beautiful, glossy, oak mantle was affixed above it. He remembered the love and care Victoria put into oiling the wood regularly, and displaying portraits and shiny lanterns, ready to be used at night. Now, the mantle only held a frame which displayed his law degree.

Scattered around the perimeter of the room were a number of chairs similar to the ones in his office. There was a desk near one wall that he hoped would eventually be occupied by a secretary. Since he had just opened for business, though, he was not yet busy enough to justify hiring anyone. Besides, he was still working on reclaiming the house and making necessary renovations.

So far, he had only worked on the downstairs, making these two rooms acceptable for business use. He was also making use of the kitchen. The dining room would be next, converted into a conference room in case the need arose for such a thing. The upstairs bedrooms would have to wait a while longer.

After locking the carriage house, his thoughts turned to Olivia. Since he had free time, he decided to walk down the street, just to make sure no one was prowling around her place. As he walked, his eyes darted around, subtly checking behind trees and in shadows for anything that seemed out of the ordinary. An older couple were sitting on the porch of one house as he passed, but overall, everything seemed quiet.

James intended to walk a distance down the street, but as he reached the Martin's house, he saw that Olivia and two children were on the porch. He raised his hand to wave, and Olivia called to him, inviting him to come up.

"Good evening, Mister MacKay. I'd like to introduce you to my children. Frannie, Michael, this is Mister MacKay. He's the attorney in the house at the corner. He is a brother to your father's good friend, Edward."

"Hello, Frannie. Hello, Michael. It's very nice to meet both of you."

"Hello, sir," they both said. James was impressed by their good manners. Frannie was sitting curled up with a book on her lap in a chair near her mother, and Michael was on the steps, tossing a baseball up and catching it.

"I'm glad you were outside. I have some information to share with you if you have time."

"Yes, of course. Would you like to take a walk?" Olivia stood, then addressed the children. "Please stay on the porch. I will be right back." She smiled at them and tousled Michael's hair as she went past him.

"When you come back, will you play catch with me, Mama?" Michael pleaded.

"Of course. I promised I would. Just give me a few minutes, okay, Son?"

"Okay." Michael's disappointment trickled into his tone and spilled out onto his features, and James made a mental note to ask Olivia about him.

James waited until they reached the front sidewalk before speaking. He had not planned on revealing the plan he had with the sheriff so soon, but when he saw her, he knew he needed a valid reason for coming down the street when his place was at the corner.

Taking a deep breath, he began. "I spoke to Ben earlier today. He has called a meeting of all the deputies tonight, which is why I'm still in town. I don't want you to be frightened, so I thought it best to make you aware that there will be a guard posted near your house at all times until we catch whoever is doing this. I plan to offer my house as a base for them to use."

Olivia's eyes were filled with concern. "Do you really think that is necessary? I do not want attention drawn to us by having guards all the time. The children will be frightened."

"They will be discreet. I will know more of the plan after we meet tonight, but yes, Ben and I both feel it is important. Unfortunately, you have inadvertently become the bait for catching these rodents. I want to know what it is they hope to achieve by forcing women out of their homes, and since it is quite likely that man from this morning will return, perhaps bringing more muscle, we want to be ready. In the outlying areas, we have deputies tuned into news of men passing, leaving a wife or children unprotected. This is no different, except that since you have already been approached, our chance of catching them may have increased."

Olivia wrung her hands as they walked slowly in front of the house next to hers. Suddenly, James wished he could put his arm around her and comfort her. Wait! Where did that thought come from? He just met this woman earlier in the day, and her grief was still raw and fresh. He needed to control his thoughts better around her.

"Do you have any questions right now?"

She shook her head, "No, at least not yet. You will keep me informed, won't you?"

"Of course I will. Now, let's go play catch with your son." James smiled at her as they turned around and walked back to her house.

"Oh, I'm sure you are busy. You don't need to take the time to throw the ball with him. Besides, I'm trying to learn to be both parents, and this is something I need to work on." She smiled sadly.

James met her gaze. "Unless you simply don't want me to stay, I would really love to throw with him." James' gaze flitted to the ground. "It's been a long time since I played ball," he added quietly.

Olivia seemed to wrestle with her emotions for a few moments while she made her decision, and felt sympathy for the man who had never been able to play with his own son. "Well, then, let's ask Michael. If he wants you to, then it's fine with me."

James's smile lit his face. This is something he would have done with his own son had he lived. He played a little bit with his nieces and nephews whenever opportunity arose, but somehow, he was excited about this in a different way. Maybe because the children in his family had fathers, and these two did not. He hoped Michael was agreeable.

When they entered the yard, Michael came running with his ball in hand. "Are you ready now, Mama?" he asked excitedly.

Glancing at Olivia, James winked at her and answered him. "Here, Michael, back up and throw it to me. I want to see how strong your arm is." Leaning toward Michael and in a conspiratorial loud whisper, he said, "You wouldn't want to hurt her with a super hard throw like I think you can make, would you?"

Michael's eyes lit up as he looked to his mother for assurance. When she nodded, he ran to the other side of the yard, turned, and threw the ball to James. To James's surprise, it reached him with no problem. Michael cheered, "Nice catch, Mister MacKay! See if you can get it back to me!" James and Olivia laughed, and James, with his tongue sticking out of the side of his mouth in concentration, wound up and threw the ball back to him, making sure it landed soft enough to not hurt the young boy's hands.

For the next half hour, Michael and James tossed the ball back and forth, challenging each other with their individual special pitches. For Michael, throwing baseball was very serious business. For James, it was just plain fun. He made a show of lunging and missing on a few occasions, which caused Michael to laugh so hard he doubled over. Once, he lost his balance and rolled in the grass. James glanced over his shoulder at Olivia and found her watching him, an indiscernible look on her face.

After a while, Olivia called to Michael to bring the ball back up to the porch so that Mister MacKay could be on his way since he was such a busy man. Michael moaned in disappointment, but did as his mother told him. Truth be told, James was almost as disappointed as the child. He had really enjoyed himself and found himself hoping for more evenings like this one. He reached out and tousled Michael's hair as he walked past him.

"Michael, it's been a great pleasure playing catch with you this evening. I hope you'll let me play again soon."

"You can play with me anytime! You're not too bad at it."

Olivia hid her giggle behind a hand, and James's eyes danced, but his tone was serious. "I'm quite relieved, you know. It's been a long time since I played with someone as talented as you, and I wasn't sure if I could measure up."

"You did good for an old man, sir," was Michael's serious assessment of the situation. James' eyebrows flew to the top of his forehead as he heard Olivia's snicker. He reached out his hand to shake Michael's before the youngster turned and ran inside to put his ball away.

James finally turned to Olivia, who was having a very difficult time keeping from bursting out laughing. He smiled and shook his head. "He's quite a boy, that son of yours."

"Mister MacKay, I'm so sorry for his cheeky remarks. I certainly did not expect that from him tonight." Olivia struggled to keep her giggling under control.

"I'm just so glad he felt comfortable enough to speak his mind." James studied her face for a moment while she sobered. Then, with a gentle smile that said he understood what was not being said, he spoke softly. "I should be going. The meeting is in a short while, and I want to finish a couple of things before going uptown. Is it alright if I come by tomorrow morning to let you know more of our plan?"

"Yes, that would be perfect. And thank you so much. It's good to have neighbors we can trust."

"That it is. Good night, Olivia."

"Good night, James," came the soft reply.

As James returned home, he couldn't help but whistle a soft tune. His heart felt lighter than it had in years. It must be from having a good game of catch with a young man who had a lot of energy and a great personality. Olivia certainly was blessed to be that boy's mother.

Chapter Nine

Ben called the meeting to order. James was impressed by the number of men who had been deputized in this town. It showed a great deal of support in the community, but he had to wonder if all of them were here to help or because they wanted to know the latest gossip. Sometimes men were worse than a lot of the old ladies that James had often encountered around the circuit. He grinned.

His eyes roamed around the room. He recognized a few faces, but not all by far. Tom Zimmerman was a few years older than James and was known as a good man. He remembered him as the smithy who had outfitted his horse, Justice, with a new set of shoes just before he left town to ride the circuit. He was a big man with a lot of strength in his shoulders and arms. What used to be blond hair was now showing signs of gray on his temples and in his beard, but his blue eyes were still bright and penetrating.

Jethro Hankins owned the lumber mill where he had purchased materials to build his house all those years ago. He had been up in years back then, and James wondered if he would remember him. Regardless, he was glad to see him here. The older gentleman was showing his age, stooped and gray, but alert and, as usual, more than willing to defend and protect his town.

James was surprised to see Angus McMahon in this group of deputies. He and Angus had been friends since they were children in school. What surprised James was that Angus was such a meek and mild man, gentle and kind to everyone. Since returning to town, James had learned that Angus had become the pastor of the local church. That fact had not surprised him.

It's not that James didn't think Angus could handle the duties of a deputy, he was certain he could. But Angus only ever carried a gun when it was absolutely necessary, like when his mother sent him hunting with James to get meat to smoke for winter, or if a varmint was invading her garden.

James smiled to himself as he recalled the time he came upon poor Angus trying to kill the chicken his mother asked him to butcher for dinner. As he approached McMahon's backyard, he heard Angus talking to himself. Except, he wasn't talking just to himself. He was holding the chicken in his outstretched hands, telling it that he did not want to kill it, and that if he had his way, he would let it go, but he was forced to punish it because of its behavior recently, scratching in his mother's garden and eating the seeds she had just sewn, hoping for a bountiful crop later in the summer.

Angus had even quoted scripture to it, saying, "Listen here, you know you did wrong. You sinned against my momma, and the Bible tells us that the wages of sin is death. Now, I don't want to be the one to mete out punishment, but I don't really have any choice, here. So, I'm going to have to kill ya, see?" What happened next astonished the silent, slack-jawed onlooker. Angus grabbed the chicken with one hand around its neck and swung it around over his head like a lasso, while the chicken flapped its wings and squawked. Finally noticing James, he tucked the chicken under his arm and sighed in relief. "James, oh thank God! I can't do it. I cannot kill this chicken. It's been in trouble in Mama's garden, and she wants it for dinner, but I just can't do it. You're going to have to do it for me."

Remembering that day, James caught himself as he met the man's eyes, just as mirth began to bubble out of his chest. A happy smile of recognition lit Angus' face, and James was sure he had been caught in the memory. Later, they would share a good laugh as they talked about old times.

Just then, the door opened, admitting a latecomer. To James's surprise, it was his youngest brother. Colin slid into a seat near the back of the room, not having seen James seated near Ben at the front. Ben had just been making general comments, but the arrival of Colin seemed to be what he was waiting on to start the meeting.

"Now that I believe we are all here, let's get started. Earlier today, a matter of grave concern was brought to my attention. Rather than making you all listen to me ramble, I'm going to ask Judge James MacKay to come tell you what this is about. Some of you know him, and those of you who don't, you need to make his acquaintance. James has been a circuit judge for a number of years but is now settling back into our town to practice law. James, come on up here and tell these fine men what you told me earlier today."

"Thank you, Ben. In my last few months on the circuit, it came to the attention of the marshals and sheriffs that some unsavory characters were victimizing individuals who had recently lost a loved one. As far as we know, all the victims were women. These bandits use fear as their motivator. At first, all we heard were whispers of the problem, but when I learned from a dear elderly lady that it was true, we deputized more men to help keep a watch out for the culprits. Here's what we know is happening: a well-dressed man goes to the home of a grieving widow and shows her some documents, stating that her home is in violation of some ordinance.

"This, of course, is completely false. I have confirmed with Judge Gray in Greensboro that there is no such ordinance. They are telling these poor women that their home can be brought up to code at no cost to themselves simply by letting one of their men do the "work" in exchange for room and board for the duration of the project. What we think is happening is they keep finding things "wrong" to prolong the stay, or in some other way make the poor woman so uncomfortable and afraid that she abandons her home. Buried in the last page of the document they want her to sign, it says that if she abandons the property, she forfeits ownership."

The sound of men's voices started rumbling through the room. James raised his hand to quiet them down. Questions started coming, one right after another, but he continued to speak. "Conveniently, the ladies are not given a chance to read the documents. In fact, there has only been one that I know of who had the opportunity to even keep the papers, and that's because she outsmarted the bandit." James smiled as he remembered the feisty Mrs. Fields.

"So, you are undoubtedly wondering why we are here tonight. This morning, a lady came to my office. She had been approached last week in the cemetery by a man claiming to have lost his wife. This morning, a different man knocked on her door with documents, telling her the same story as I've just shared with you. Her home is in immaculate condition, and even if such an ordinance existed, she would not be in violation. He insisted she sign the papers, but when she wanted to read them, he grabbed them back from her just as she slammed the door in his face. After she stopped shaking, she came to me for advice."

In the back corner of the room, near where Colin was seated, James noticed one man looking furtively around at the other men. He seemed a little nervous. James noticed he held a dark coat, and hadn't spoken up, even to ask questions, unlike all the other men. He memorized the man's looks and made a mental note to ask Ben who he was and where he lived. He would need to vet these deputies himself, if only for his own peace of mind. He wanted to be sure no one would harm Olivia and her children.

Tom Zimmerman spoke up, asking the question burning in the minds of all the men present. "James, what is the plan, then? How are we goin' ta catch these mongrels?"

Ben stepped forward, thanking James. "I've asked you all here tonight so we can set up a schedule to guard Olivia Martin's house around the clock. We don't think these men are violent, but then, to our knowledge, they have not been crossed, so we are not entirely sure what they are capable of. Also, we don't know what their motive is for obtaining these properties. Might be just so they can sell them for a hefty profit. They are well dressed, and so far, all reports have them wearing long dark coats. James has dubbed them "the property bandits." Seems pretty fitting to me. So, for the sake of this project, that's what we will call them. Any questions before we assign time slots?"

Men began talking all at once, and Ben answered the questions he was able to hear. Eventually, James spoke up again. "Since Missus Martin lives on my street, I would like to offer my office as a central meeting area. Her house is only four away from mine, and since mine is a business, a casual observer won't find it strange seeing men coming and going during the day.

"Each team can debrief the next, until we catch these criminals. One thing is of utmost importance: discretion is key. She does not want her children upset. Anyone on guard duty must remain unseen. I will arrange for there to be food and water available for each shift. All communication with her must go through me, and since I have met the children and they know I own the house at the corner, they will not question my presence on their porch."

After another half hour of discussing details of the plan and sorting the schedule, men began filing out or standing in clusters to talk about the latest news. James looked up to find his brother approaching. He returned Colin's smile with one of his own, and they greeted one another with a warm embrace.

"How did you come to be deputized, little brother? And why did I not know this?"

"I've been deputized for several years now, since I returned from the war. Figure I have training, might as well use it to help protect my hometown."

"Well, I'm mighty proud of you for doing that, Colin. How's Mary? Is she feeling well these days?" Colin's wife was expecting their first child and had had a rough few months. He knew that Colin was nervous about it, but the doctor had assured him all would be well.

"She's been feeling a lot better recently. Doc says she's past the worst part now. I'm not so sure. Seems like the birthing will be worse. Or maybe the years following the birth," he added with a laugh, which James shared.

"So, Missus Martin. She's a looker, isn't she?" The twinkling glint in Colin's eyes gave away his teasing.

"She's my client. And a neighbor." James shot him a glare meant to quiet the teasing, but it didn't quite have the punch he intended. Instead, all it did was cause his brother to laugh.

"Whatever you say, big brother. But you've already met the children, huh?"

"I thought I'd just walk past her house to check on things before I came here. They happened to be in the front yard, and she invited me up to meet the children. Since I was there, I told her about our plan, then played a little catch with Michael. Poor kid is missing his pa something awful. Olivia is struggling to fill the role of both parents. I was glad to be of some help for a few minutes."

Colin stared at him for a few moments before he spoke. "Olivia? Hmm. And you just met her this morning?"

James' cheeks flushed pink when he realized how that sounded. "Well, er, yes, I mean... Well, we are neighbors, so it seems logical to be friendly. Besides, her late husband was Edward's good friend. It's not that ridiculous, so stop looking at me like that."

Colin threw his head back and laughed, causing James to roll his eyes. In an attempt to change the topic, he asked Colin what shift he hoped to draw. They talked more about the case, James filling Colin in with more detail than he had in the public meeting. He was glad to see his brother had a good mind for law enforcement, and wondered if he would ever pursue that career path.

"I know you want to take a shift, too, James, but maybe you should stand back and do like you said, be the liaison between us and Missus Martin. What do you think, Ben?" The man had just walked over to them and nodded his head in agreement.

"He's right, James. We need you to keep an eye open, of course, but from a distance. Someone watching would just think you are visiting a neighbor, or client. Of course, you could be seeing her in another capacity. That would certainly help protect her and her children, but it might not help us catch the bandits." James caught a wink Ben sent to Colin.

Great! Now there were two of them teasing him. Poor Olivia didn't know what she was up against. These men were worse than a couple of old hens playing matchmaker.

He should have been furious with them, but somehow, he couldn't. What in the world did that mean?!

Chapter Ten

The next morning, James sat up slowly, trying to work the kinks out of his back and neck. He decided sleeping on a hard floor was worse than sleeping on the ground. At least grass was softer than wood. He might have to consider getting a thick rug. Maybe he could borrow one from the plantation for the duration of his time here overseeing Olivia's guards. But, for now, it was time to make a fresh pot of coffee and see what he could rustle up for breakfast for himself and any of the men coming and going.

Last night had been pretty quiet. Before going to bed, he walked down past Olivia's house again. Everything had been dark and quiet, putting his mind at ease. He didn't really expect anything to go wrong during the night, but one could never be too careful.

Especially since he still had no idea what these men were up to.

Besides selling off properties for a handsome profit, what could they be after? James had wracked his brain, trying to invent reasons for this kind of activity. A person needed to think like a criminal to devise a plan, but in spite of the number of lawbreakers he had encountered over his years as a judge, this puzzled him, and it irritated his normally even disposition.

He went through the motions of frying some bacon and eggs to share with the guard who would soon come in from the overnight assignment. He thought back to the meeting last night, going over in his mind the different men who were assigned time slots. He counted eight, so that meant there were four he didn't know. Most of them were younger than him, meaning they would have been not much more than children when he left.

He scratched his jaw, wondering about the man in the back near where Colin had sat. Something about that man didn't sit right with him, and he was determined to figure out what it was. He wondered when Colin would be on the job and hoped it would be soon. Perhaps they could sit awhile on his porch and have coffee and a chat.

Before he could think about it further, the front door opened, and he heard footsteps coming through the house to the kitchen.

"Is coffee ready?" James was pleasantly surprised to find that his brother was approaching him.

"Freshly made, little brother. Grab a cup and help yourself. Breakfast will be done in a minute."

"Good! I'm starving! Those were some long hours overnight. I came in between two and three and heard you snoring. I don't know how you slept on the floor. You're not so young anymore!" Colin teased. James had almost forgotten that his youngest brother had been blessed with an abundance of charming sass, so the teasing was mostly tolerated by the whole family.

"You just wait, you'll be this old soon enough! I plan to go out to the plantation today to see if Mama has a thick rug or blankets I can borrow for a while."

"Why don't you bring a bed? Is the upstairs so uninhabitable that you couldn't sleep there?"

"I suppose I could. I just wasn't ready to move that much furniture in here yet. It would be in the way of making the repairs that are needed."

"Even just a mattress on the floor would be a help to you. Easily moved when you need to. With all the empty rooms at the plantation house, I'm sure you could borrow one." Colin poured his coffee and turned, leaning against the counter.

James took the last of the eggs out of the skillet. "Help yourself. Got time to sit on the porch with it?"

"Sure, I can spare you some time. Mary was up early to see me off with a full belly several hours ago, and I told her to get back into bed and stay there until I returned. Hope she feels alright today."

James smiled, remembering when Victoria was experiencing those same symptoms. After the first few months, though, it seemed that she glowed, and becoming a mother looked good on her. They had anticipated the birth of their baby with so much joy.

How had it all gone so wrong in the end? Sometimes the sadness still tried to choke him, even after fifteen years.

When they both had filled their plates and cups, they walked out onto the front porch just as the sun was peeking over the horizon. Even though the house was in town, it sat on just enough of a hill to enable a view over other houses. In this neighborhood, the homes had more space between them than in other areas of town, which made the view better. James was glad that had not changed too much since he had lived here. Still, he made sure to position himself in a way that he could see as much as possible of the front of Olivia's house from his vantage point.

"I didn't get to look at the schedule last night, but I know Tom was on first. Obviously, you relieved him. Who relieved you?" James asked after he'd enjoyed a few bites of a hot breakfast.

"Angus is down there now." Colin took a sip of his coffee.

"I meant to ask Ben last night, but maybe you can tell me. Who was the man sitting in back near you? I've never seen him before."

Colin frowned, then remembered. "That's Aerick Reicher. He's only been in the area about a year. Bought a place about an hours' ride west of town. It had been abandoned, and he said he got a good deal on it." He took another bite of eggs and broke off a piece of bacon and popped it into his mouth, too; then, talking around the mouthful, he added, "Don't know too much about him other than that."

James was quiet, eyebrows drawn, scratching his chin with the tip of his fork handle. Something about that seemed strange to him. "Do you know when he is on the schedule?"

"Not sure. Sometimes he comes to meetings, but this is the first time we've had someone to guard around the clock like this. Since he lives so far out, he may not be able to get here to do it and still take care of his place. He runs cattle out there. Pretty big spread if I recall. Like I said, it's quite a distance out of town." Colin finally seemed to notice James' thoughtful look, and asked slowly, "What are you thinking?"

"I just had an uneasy feeling when I saw him last night. He acted kind of nervous, and that doesn't cotton with the job of a deputy. I'm concerned that he was on a hunting expedition, and now, instead of helping protect, he's gone to warn the others that we're onto them. It's just a hunch right now, but I'm planning to go have a word with Ben this morning. What about the others? I know Tom, Jethro, and Angus. And of course you." He turned and smiled at Colin.

James was sure he had made the right decision in getting out of the circuit. He had missed all of this youngest brother's growing up years. He had still been so young when James left, and his infrequent visits had not been long enough to really know this brother who was now a man. Besides that, Colin had been away fighting in the war for several of those years. He looked forward to times ahead to reconnect with the older siblings, and to really know the younger ones.

He listened intently as Colin described the other three men. Each of them sounded like solid men of the community, coming from families who had been around for generations. James recognized the family names of each of them, but knew that, even though a man isn't guaranteed to be like his parents, the probability of him having similar character was strong.

"I recognize those men. Not personally, of course, but I know of their families, and as such, I have no real concerns about them. That other one, though...whew!" James shook his head. He could not shake the feeling that something was off with that man.

They talked a while longer, sipping coffee, and reminiscing about things from their childhood. James looked down toward Olivia's house and saw Angus on the other side of the street coming toward them. A smile stretched his face, glad he would finally have a chance to catch up with his old friend. Colin saw his smile and turned to see what had captured his attention.

"I expected to see a lovely young lady coming along by the way your face brightened," he teased.

"Nah, just an old friend that I'm looking forward to seeing again."

"I didn't realize you knew him so well."

"Yes, we were childhood friends. We made a lot of memories together." James chuckled as the memory of the chicken played through his mind again. He caught Colin looking at him as if he were crazy.

"I need to get home and check on Mary so I can go to work." Colin stood, gathered his dishes and James' plate, and took them inside to the kitchen. After quickly washing them, he came out the front door just as Angus was climbing the steps onto the porch. The two men shook hands, and Colin went around to the stable next to the carriage house to collect his horse. Then, tipping his hat to the other two men, he rode out of town.

***

Olivia stood on her porch watching Frannie and Michael walking down the street toward school. She sighed, thinking how different things would be if Peter was still alive. As much as she had not wanted to frighten them, she knew she needed to remind them to be careful around strangers. Should she have gone into more detail and explained why this reminder was coming now? She shook her head, reluctant to believe they were in danger of losing more than their home if these men came back with a threat. No, a simple reminder to stay together and come straight home after school would have to do for now.

    That led her into thinking about how easy it had been for her to open up to James the day before. Maybe it was the warmth of his hazel eyes that reduced her inhibitions. He was so kind, not only to her, but to her children, also. A smile formed on her face as she remembered him playing catch with Michael. He had actually been enjoying it. And it had been good for Michael, too. He would be the one to suffer most by not having his father around to teach him things a young man needed to know.

Maybe James would be willing to take Michael on as an apprentice of sorts. Not in his law practice, necessarily, but more as someone to mentor him as he grows up. For things like fishing trips and campouts, building and fixing things, interacting with other men and learning social graces. All the things his father should be doing with him.

Olivia took a shuddering breath and released it as she turned to go back into the house, wiping the lone tear that trickled down her cheek. Later, she would take a walk, maybe head over to the cemetery and have another talk with Peter. Meanwhile, she needed to wash up from breakfast and start some bread to go with the stew she planned to make for dinner.

As she moved about her tasks, her mind went back to things that had happened yesterday. Was it really just yesterday that her home had been threatened by the man in the dark coat? He had seemed so congenial at first, until she insisted on reading the contract he showed her. How quickly his eyes turned cold and his whole demeanor changed when she challenged him!

She was so relieved to have found James, that he had believed her, and had not made her feel silly for her fears. He had known exactly what to do to keep her and her children safe. If she had not seen his sign up just the day before, she would have gone to the sheriff, but she hadn't had many encounters with the man and didn't know how he would have reacted.

James had saved her from that, too. Of course, he was a man who had connections and knew how to get things done. Still, she was so grateful that he was willing to put his own work aside and speak to the sheriff on her behalf.

It was interesting to her that she had not seen any of the deputies in her neighborhood. Maybe they hadn't been around last night or yet this morning; or maybe the sheriff decided the situation was not serious enough that it merited guarding them after all. James had been sure that there would be someone on duty, but that didn't mean it would be all night and all day. Surely the man in the dark coat was only likely to come back during the day, anyway.

As Olivia finished drying and putting away breakfast dishes, she wondered what James would have to say when she saw him. She grinned as she found herself looking forward to seeing him again; after all, he was quite handsome and charming. In spite of how yesterday began, she'd laughed more than she had in months. He had made her feel safe, and when he smiled at her, she hadn't wanted to admit it, but her cheeks warmed, and she felt like a young girl again.

Then, feeling guilty, she scolded herself. *Olivia, what are you thinking! He is only a neighbor, an attorney who is helping you solve a problem. Just because he was nice to you and played ball with your son does not mean he wants more to do with you than that. He's just a nice man! Besides, Peter hasn't been gone very long. God has punished you for falling short, and you don't deserve anyone else.*

Before she could form another thought, she grabbed her shawl and went out the front door. She wasn't sure where she was headed, but she needed a brisk walk this morning. At the end of her sidewalk, she automatically turned toward where Maple met Main Street. She let her feet lead her, and eventually she found herself at the entrance to the cemetery. Apparently, now was the time to have that talk with Peter.

Chapter Eleven

James finished the breakfast clean-up, checked that his hair and beard looked presentable, put on his hat, and went out onto the porch. He smiled and hummed a tune, thinking about seeing Olivia soon. Was she perhaps the answer to his recent prayer? He knew that she was still feeling the rawness of grief from the loss of her husband, but he could be patient, take his time getting to know her and the children, and just be their friend.

He tried to put himself in her shoes. Knowing how emotionally dependent his wife had been on him, he could imagine that Olivia felt the same way. Of course, she would be protective of her children, too. He hadn't had children to consider after Victoria died, which is why he had been able to sell his house and leave town. Maybe he had been a coward, running from his grief instead of facing it.

All things considered, though, his career had been blessed. He had done a lot of good for the mountain towns and mining camps, and he had met a lot of wonderful people on his journey. He didn't regret any of it, unless it was the fact that he missed out on so much around the plantation with his family. Still, he had visited as often as possible; now, his little sister's wedding was next weekend, and he looked forward to the event with great excitement. He couldn't wait to see his brothers and sisters, nieces and nephews all together again. Besides, knowing Emily Rose was so much in love with Jacob made his heart happy.

As he descended the steps to the sidewalk, he glanced down Main Street. A woman was walking briskly toward the outskirts of town. She looked an awful lot like Olivia, so instead of going toward her house as he had intended, he followed her, hoping there was nothing wrong. Angus was still on guard duty and would have reported if the property bandits had been there already this morning, but he wanted to check with her to be sure everything was okay.

He took off at a jog, but by the time he almost caught up to her, she turned and went into the cemetery. Feeling foolish, he slowed his steps, wondering what he should do now. It might seem callous of him to follow her in, but he was concerned enough to continue on and make sure she was okay. Maybe he would just stay by the gate and keep watch. It wouldn't do to have her accosted in the cemetery again.

When he sensed her coming back toward the gate, he looked up. She was walking slowly, and he wondered what she was thinking. Trying not to intrude, he turned and looked up the street toward town until he heard her sharp intake of breath.

"Mister MacKay! What are you doing here? You startled me! Did you follow me here?" she asked in surprise.

"I was just heading toward your house when I thought I saw you coming this direction. I just wanted to ensure that nothing had happened. You seemed to be in a hurry, and I was concerned. Is everything okay?"

"Yes. Everything is fine, thank you. You didn't need to check up on me." She raised her chin proudly and set off purposefully toward home, and he fell into step next to her. "Why were you coming to my house?"

"If you remember, last night I said I would come by today to tell you what had been decided at the meeting of the deputies."

He was watching her face and noticed the brief look of surprise, followed by resignation.

"Right. I had forgotten, please forgive me."

"Nothing to forgive. I'm sure you have a lot on your mind."

"Yes." She took a deep breath. "So, what did you find out?"

"We agreed that someone would be watching your house around the clock. We intend to catch these culprits and put a stop to their illegal activity."

"When will it start? I need to warn my children so they won't be alarmed."

James grinned. "It already has."

Her surprise made him chuckle. "I haven't seen anyone."

"Exactly. That's the plan. We don't want the bandits to know we are watching for them."

"Are you one of the guards?"

"No, my job is much more enjoyable." James smiled, eyes crinkling at the corners. She couldn't help but smile at the mischief she saw lurking behind his eyes.

"And what is that, exactly?"

"I get to be your friend, and the liaison between you and the guards. My house is their home base where the shift change happens, where the deputies will report to one another, and a place to get food or coffee. They can sit on the porch to rest while still watching, and because it is also a place of business, no one will be the wiser. I will be a safe haven for you and your children, so anytime you feel afraid or threatened, or if you have any questions or concerns, you can come to me, okay?"

Olivia's fingers twisted around each other while she thought about that. James wondered what was going through her mind, and whether she would resist the help he was trying to offer. After a few moments, she finally spoke.

"What will people say? I'm sure someone has already noticed that we are walking together now. Tongues will be wagging, I'm sure." Her jaw clenched.

"Does it bother you that much? We are simply walking down the street together."

She looked up at him incredulously. "Yes! Because just being in public with you feels like I am cheating on Peter. People won't understand. I don't intend for anyone to find out about the threats, but with you being new in town, most people don't know you and would not know that you are just protecting us within the law." She forced out a frustrated breath, and James thought he saw moisture in the corner of her eye.

His voice softened, and he caught himself before stretching a protective arm around her shoulders. "I'm sorry this is so upsetting. Maybe I should not have followed you, but I was worried that something had happened again."

"I understand, and I'm not angry with you. I'm just angry! Angry that Peter left me, angry that I have to deal with all this alone, angry that these men have threatened my home. It makes me feel more vulnerable than I ever have, and it's frightening. Will these feelings ever end? Will I ever feel safe again? Will the emptiness subside?" Her voice faltered and she swiped away a tear that threatened to roll down her cheek.

He took her arm and stopped her, turning toward her slightly. "Olivia, you are not alone. I know it feels like it right now, but the sheriff and deputies are working to find these men. You did a good thing yesterday, coming and telling me about what happened. You do not have to deal with it alone, because I'm here to help you in any way you need. And, I completely understand the feeling of being left alone. Why do you think I left town for fifteen years? I couldn't face being here, seeing all the familiar faces every day, and coming home to an empty house only to not see that one face that I desperately wanted to see. My options were more open at that time than yours are now, but I still took the coward's way out. You have your children to consider, so of course it's more complicated. Add to that the threats, and I can't imagine how that feels for you. But you are not alone. Please. Let me help you."

"But you have your own life. You don't need us to tie you down. We'll be fine."

James wondered what else he could do to convince her that he truly wanted to help, that it was in no way a hardship or obligation. He shoved down the feeling of wanting to do more. The time was not right. After all, they had just met yesterday. He didn't want to cause problems for her among her friends and neighbors. And she was right: most people didn't yet know him.

They had reached Maple Street, where his house and office sat on the corner. Everything in him wanted to walk with her to her front door, but to preserve her independence, he hesitated before crossing the street to his sidewalk.

"Promise me that anytime you need something, you let me know, okay? You can send one of the children to get me. I'll be here whenever you need me."

She paused, looking up at him. He noticed the shine of unshed tears in her eyes, and he wanted to hold her and let her cry.

"I appreciate your friendship, James. Thank you."

Smiling warmly, he said, "You're welcome, Olivia," and he watched her walk away, only turning toward his own sidewalk when she had reached hers.

***

James was lost in thought as he ascended the steps to his office. Clouds threatened rain, so it wouldn't be prudent to work outside on one of the big projects he still had to do. Instead, he decided it might be a good idea to take a trip out to the plantation and bring back a bed. He wished he could ask Olivia to come with him. It would ensure her safety and keep the bandits from approaching her while he was gone. But on the other hand, the bandits *needed* to approach her again so they could be arrested.

James balled his fists in frustration. Never in his life had he wanted to punch someone as much as he wanted to right now. He had never been a violent person; instead, he had been the peacemaker. This strong emotion surprised and puzzled him. Why was he reacting so, and for a woman he barely knew? Yes, she was attractive, with her honey blonde hair, her sad blue eyes, and feminine curves he should not be noticing. He had enjoyed talking to her and playing catch with Michael, but why did he want to do everything in his power to protect and take care of them? He knew a lot of people, many of them widows, but he didn't recall ever reacting to any of them like this.

After checking in with the guard who was about to take over for Angus, James saddled Justice and headed to the plantation. It would be good to have a change of scenery for a little while. He had spent a lot of daytime hours in town recently, working on his house, turning it into an office, so it would be good to visit with his parents during the day, and the ride would give him some time to think.

As he passed the cemetery, he recalled the events of this morning. He knew Olivia visited Peter's grave often, and his heart broke for her, knowing she missed her husband desperately. It made him think back to the months following Victoria's death. He remembered feeling like his life had ended, he was so brokenhearted.

People told him it would get better, but he had not believed them. For a while. Then, one day, after having a long talk with God and being reminded that by turning his eyes to Him, he would be comforted, he realized the pain had dulled, and he could recall events and conversations with her with a smile instead of tears and anger.

He always knew that God was his strength and comfort, but it took time until he fully understood it. After fifteen years, he still missed what his life could have been had she not died, but the pain was gone, and only occasional sadness remained. He hoped he could be of help to Olivia in her journey of grief. No one understood it better than he did.

After taking care of Justice and releasing him into the corral, he went in search of his father. Henry was in his study near the front door of the house. When he saw James, he came around the desk and greeted his son with a warm embrace.

"I'm surprised to see ye here in the middle of the day, lad. How are things going with the house? We missed ye last evening."

"It's coming along. I fixed the carriage house door yesterday. Now I need to get a carriage to put in it!" James laughed and took a seat across from his Pa's desk. "I need to gather a few more tools to take back with me. I find myself in need of tree trimming equipment, too."

"I thought your trees were in good condition. Did a storm break a branch?"

"Actually, a neighbor needs a branch cut before it reaches a window on the back of the house."

"And he doesn't have the tools to do it? That seems unusual. Is he new to the neighborhood or young and inexperienced?"

"*She* is certainly inexperienced, and I thought I should lend a hand."

Henry's eyes twinkled in mischief. "*She*, huh? Aye, I'd say ye should lend a hand, lad." Seeing the color creep up on James's neck, he burst into laughter just as Catherine came into the study.

"What am I missing? I thought I heard an extra voice. I wondered if my dear Henry was talking to himself again," she said with a wink and smile at her husband. "James, what a lovely surprise. What brings you here in the middle of the day? Is everything alright? Are you hungry?"

James laughed. "Ma, you know I'm always ready to eat, especially when it comes to yours and Cookie's cooking. I came to gather a few supplies, tools and such, and wondered if I could borrow a bed for a while."

"You know you can always stay, don't be silly, Son."

"I meant to take to the house in town. I need to stay there for a while. It has to do with a case I've taken on, and I'm not sure how long I'll need to be there. Last night I slept on the floor and found out pretty quickly that I'm not as young as I once was." James pulled a face and rubbed his neck dramatically for emphasis. His parents laughed.

"Of course, take whatever you need. You know there are several empty beds in this house. Come to the dining room for lunch, now, both of you. Then maybe you can tell us a little bit about this case you're working on."

Catherine waited until Henry came around the desk to join her, then, with their arms around each other, they led the way to the dining room. An ache formed in the pit of James' stomach, and he realized it was a longing to have that kind of relationship again. They had always been such great examples of what a couple should look like, and he knew he could not settle for anything less than true love.

He knew a lot of people in his situation had married for convenience, but that had never seemed right to him. Yes, he missed the companionship he once had with Victoria, but he had never considered marrying just to have someone cook for him and someone to talk to. When - if - he married again, it would be for love, for the simple fact that he could not imagine another day without seeing her, talking to her, holding her. So why did Olivia's face come to mind? James shook himself mentally and prepared for a nice meal and visit with his parents.

Chapter Twelve

Olivia decided that the best way to expel some of her frustration and anger was to take it out on her rugs, so she rolled up the one in the parlor and dragged it outside. After hoisting it up over the clothesline, she grabbed her rug-beater and began beating it as hard as she could, all the while alternately yelling at Peter and allowing tears to flow unchecked.

How could you leave me like this? (whack!) I've never felt so alone in my life! (whack!) You were my shield and protector against men who prey on women. (whack!) These people who want our house might be just the beginning. (whack!) What if they want more from me? (whack!) What am I supposed to do? (whack!) We were a team! (whack!) Partners! (whack!) I don't want to go through the rest of my life alone and vulnerable and afraid. (whack!) How am I supposed to protect our children when I feel this way? I can't do this, Peter! I know that the Bible says God will fulfill all my needs, but it doesn't feel like He can fill the hole you left in my heart. It's like half of me is missing and never coming back. I just.... can't!

Sobbing, she allowed the rug beater to slip from her grasp. Olivia buried her face in her hands and let her hot, angry, heart-broken tears fall as she dropped onto the grass. She tried to pray, but the words would not come. Eventually, she moved to the back porch and sat down on the step and just let the emotions roll over her. Would it ever get better? People seemed to think it would, but she just could not imagine how.

She still woke up during the night, reaching for him, only to find his side of the bed cold and empty. She found a small amount of comfort from hugging his pillow, but his scent had already dissipated. Sometimes she went to the wardrobe and buried her face in his shirts that hung there, but they smelled of fresh air and sunshine instead of the scent that was his.

In her anger, she went to the room they had shared and quickly gathered all his belongings, folding them into a box she had retrieved from the attic. Maybe it was time to accept that he would not need his things any longer. Maybe the pain would ease when she didn't have to look at everything of his that remained stationary, never moving from one spot to another. Maybe it would be better to give them to someone who could actually use them.

Once the wardrobe and bureau drawers were emptied of his clothing, she closed the boxes, took them to the carriage house, and placed them in the back of the wagon. Then she found one more small box and put all his personal belongings in it, things like his razor, his wallet, a couple of books, a few photos, and anything else that was strictly his. Her thought was that one day Frannie and Michael would want to see them or have them. She never wanted them to forget who he was.

As she was cleaning out the drawer of his bedside table, she found a few letters they had written to each other when they were courting. Reading them now, she decided she was not ready to pack those away yet. A teardrop fell onto the paper, blurring a word. No, these she would keep in her room to bring out whenever she needed to hear him speaking to her. His words would remind her of the way he had always made her feel cherished, and maybe that would help fill the hole in her heart, giving her the strength to keep going.

Tying a ribbon around the letters and putting them back in the drawer, she prayed again. *Lord, I'm trying to trust you. I don't understand why you took Peter away from us so soon. I guess you needed him with you more than we needed him to stay, but it doesn't make any sense to me. How is it better for Frannie and Michael to be without a father? How is it better for me to be alone to face all the challenges of home and family without my partner? What am I missing? What am I being punished for? Did I not love him well enough?*

People have told me that it would be best for me to find a new husband, but I can't imagine that. Is that what you want for me? Is that what Peter would have wanted? I remember on a few occasions when we talked about 'what if', he told me I would find someone, but I said I could never do that. Now that I'm facing my life alone, I'm wondering if that's what I have to do. I'm filled with fear, thanks to the man who came to my door, and I feel unprotected. And my children need someone who would love them like a father would. But what kind of man would want someone else's children? Show me your plan, Lord. I can't see it on my own. Help me know what you want me to do!

***

As Olivia went about her chores the rest of the day, she realized that her heart was lighter than it had been in quite some time. She found herself humming melodies that they sang in church, some of them from her childhood.

Remember Ruth?

Olivia whirled around from the kitchen sink, but didn't see anyone. Who said that? Her heart was pounding in her chest as she picked up a sharp knife and slowly walked toward the front of the house.

I gave her a kinsman redeemer. I will also provide for you.

"Ok," Olivia thought out loud. "Am I going crazy? I'm hearing voices now. What is going on?" She continued to search the house, but finding no one inside, she went out onto the front porch, frantically looking for the guard who was supposedly nearby.

She must have looked sufficiently panicked, because one of the deputies materialized on the sidewalk across the street. He was an older gentleman with a walking stick who appeared to be casually strolling along, but when she made eye contact with him, he came toward her.

Quietly, he asked, "Everything ok, Missus Martin?"

"Have you seen anyone, Mister Hankins? I thought I heard someone speaking to me, but I'm here alone."

"No ma'am, I haven't. Been keepin' a close eye, just like we was told."

"Hmm I must be hearing things then. I was sure someone was in the kitchen with me."

"I'll take a walk around the perimeter of the house just to make sure. You go on back inside. I'll let you know if I see anything unusual."

"Thank you," Olivia replied. Her trembling hand reached for the doorknob to let herself back into the house.

Wobbly knees lowered her body into an overstuffed chair. She sank back and closed her eyes, feeling like she was going mad. What was going on? Why was she hearing someone who seemingly wasn't even there? Had she imagined it? Who could it have been?

After the shock had sufficiently faded, she made her way back to the kitchen to finish her cleaning, but she continued to feel anxious about everything that had happened that day. Idly, she wondered what James would say if she told him she was hearing things. She scoffed at the notion. Why would she think he would be someone to talk to about such a thing? He would probably have her locked up and her children taken away!

No, best to just keep her nonsensical thoughts to herself. There must be a rational explanation for hearing a voice in her kitchen. She had been so busy today that she must have exhausted herself. That had to be it. But was it *truly* a voice she had heard? Thinking back on it, she wasn't sure if it was male or female. Was it more of a whisper? She couldn't be sure, although at the time, it had certainly seemed audible.

Was it Peter's voice speaking to her? Even with all the trips to the cemetery to talk to him, she had never felt like he was engaging in a conversation with her. This was not really a voice she recognized, and yet it seemed familiar. Maybe if she concentrated on placing it, she would hear it again and solve the mystery.

***

James hitched Justice to the wagon he had borrowed from the barn and loaded the tools and furniture he was taking with him. He was anxious to get back into town. He hadn't liked leaving for so long, not knowing what might be going on around Olivia's house. He hoped the culprit would show his face again today and that the deputies on duty would be able to apprehend him and end the trouble, but he was worried about Olivia.

During lunch, he had told his parents about the situation, explaining the pattern these men seemed to be following. He talked about Gretchen and Missus Fields and his conversations with Matt and Nathan. As he told them about what Olivia described to him yesterday, he felt a surge of protection rising up in his chest, and the urgency to return to town to check on her and her house.

He caught the looks his parents had exchanged with one another. In past years, he would have been annoyed that anyone even thought that he might be interested in someone again, but he realized that this time it didn't bother him at all. He paused as he tied a tarp over the furniture on the wagon and frowned, wondering why his reaction was different this time.

He tried to convince himself that he was simply concerned for a neighbor who happened to be recently widowed, and because they had something in common, why should he not help her? Why shouldn't he watch out for her safety? Besides, wasn't it his job as a member of law enforcement to make sure the culprits were caught and dealt with according to the letter of the law?

After bidding farewell to his parents, he climbed aboard the wagon and signaled the horse to move. All the way back to town, he thought about how he was responding to Olivia. Could it be that God had led him back here at this particular time for a specific reason? What was that reason? Was it simply to help with apprehending the criminals and stopping their activity from hurting women like Olivia?

Or was it more than that? What was it about this particular woman that made him want to go beyond the scope of his responsibility? He thought about how much he had enjoyed being with her and her children the previous evening. Was that it? Was it simply the fact that he was missing the blessing of having a family?

He would have to be careful not to assume their sudden presence in his life was a sign. It would be too easy to fall, but that wouldn't be fair to any of them. Just because he liked what he saw didn't mean she felt the same. And just because that little boy wanted to play with him didn't mean he could or should step into the role his father had so recently vacated.

James sighed. *Lord, guide my steps. Help me not get so caught up with trying to protect what isn't mine that I miss the blessings you have for me. Help me know what I need to do for Olivia as her friend. And if You put her into my life for more than that, let us both know when it is right.*

When he rolled up into his yard, Ben was just dismounting and leading his horse into the stable. Good. He needed to talk to him anyway, so he was glad to see he would be able to do that without tracking him down in town. Maybe the man would help him carry the things he brought with him into the house.

As he walked around the wagon untying the tarp, he looked down the street to Olivia's house and wondered if there had been any activity while he was gone. A familiar figure came toward him on his side of the street, and he recognized Jethro Hankins. He waved and smiled as the older gentleman came into the yard.

"Howdy, James!"

"Hello, there, Mister Hankins!"

"Now, young man, don't you know when you call me Mister it makes me feel old? It's Jethro! Especially now as you're gettin' a few gray hairs on your temples."

Self-consciously, James touched his hand to his head and they both laughed as Ben joined them near the wagon.

"What'cha got there, James? Need some help unloading it?"

"I was hoping you could give me a hand. I went to the plantation and brought a few pieces of furniture to help me get by while I'm staying here. Sleeping on the floor last night made me realize I'm not so young anymore, so I borrowed a bed and a couple other things. I'd appreciate the extra muscle to get it upstairs."

"Sure, let's do it. You timed that pretty good. Jethro, would you mind just staying a few extra minutes while we do this?"

"I'll even hold the door open for ya!" the older man replied with a chuckle.

Chapter Thirteen

Late the following week, James walked to the sheriff's office to meet with Ben. He found himself puzzled that the bandits had not returned to Olivia's house. This was not their normal pattern, from what he had been told. He also knew that Aerick Reicher had not been on the guard rotation, and even with what Colin had told him, he had reservations about the man.

"Howdy, James. Have a seat." Ben greeted him with a smile and handshake. Because of this bandit problem, they had spent quite a bit of time together and had become friends. They typically sat with a cup of coffee on James's porch anytime Ben was on guard duty, talking about everything from their families to work.

"Ben, I'm just bewildered about this whole thing. I can't believe the bandits gave up on Olivia's house so easily She's not the first one to slam the door in their faces. From what I know of their activities, they are not ones to just walk away."

"I know you're right, James. Unfortunately, I can't justify asking the men to continue their vigilance when there has been no sign of them at all."

James puffed out a breath. "I understand. They all have lives they want to get back to. I'll do the best I can to keep watch from a distance, just like I have been." He leaned forward in his chair, elbows on his thighs, tented fingers propping up his chin. "I've been meaning to ask you about one of the deputies. Colin told me his name is Aerick Reicher, and that he's new to the community. How well do you know him and how did he come to be part of your team of deputies?"

Startled, Ben's head reared back, and his eyebrows shot up. Leaning back in his chair and folding his hands over his chest, he said, "Well, I don't know him real well, to be honest. He came to me when he first bought his place. Said he wanted to know if there was anyone out his way available to help if the need came up. Said he knew that sometimes places farther away from town could become targets for outlaws. When I told him we didn't have anyone assigned to that region, he offered his services. I asked him the typical questions and once I was satisfied with his answers, swore him in. That's pretty much it. Unfortunately, being a smaller town we don't have the kind of training and such like Greensboro would. We have to just do what we can to protect people." He paused and studied James for a moment. "Why, what are you thinking?"

"Well, the night of our first meeting, he seemed a little strange to me, looking around furtively, like he was nervous about something - especially when I described the property bandits and how they were targeting women. It seemed like he skedaddled out of there pretty fast when the meeting was over. I tried to brush it off, especially when Colin told me he lives so far out of town. But I find it odd that no more contact has been made to Olivia since that first day. I know the men are staying out of sight unless they are walking along the street or sitting on my porch. Even Olivia doesn't know where they are most of the time. So why is that? Something just seems off about him, and I wonder if he's the key."

"I hadn't put that together, but it might be worth checking into. I'll take a ride out there and have a talk with him."

"Have you been to his place before?"

"No, never had the need."

"I'm wondering how he came about obtaining the property. And does he have a family or is he there alone?"

"Well, you know how it is. People buy and sell property all the time without notifying my office. Could be he just came 'round at a time right when it was put up for sale."

"Or maybe he obtained it illegally," James spoke his thoughts slowly and quietly.

Ben let out a low whistle. "Wouldn't that be something? That whole operation could be right under our noses. Yeah, definitely something I need to look into. I'll check at the land office before I go out there, see if I can dig up any information so I have an idea what I'm getting into. You know, if we didn't need you as a lawyer in town, I'd recruit you as a deputy." Ben smiled and James grinned, shaking his head.

"You know I'll do anything I can to help you, Ben, but I would prefer not getting shot at when you find the bad guys. I'd rather be the one to put them behind bars. It would give me great satisfaction to do that with this bunch."

"We'll keep the rotation until I can find out more information. I'll let you know." Ben snapped his fingers. "I just remembered, would you be available for guard duty tomorrow? One of the guys had something come up, and I've got to go help my mother with a repair on her house. I've been putting it off long enough. But if you can't, that's fine. I'll cover it."

"Well, actually, tomorrow is my little sister's wedding, but I can see if Olivia and the kids want to come with me. They are friends with some of my nieces and nephews, and Olivia knows a few of my family anyway. It would be no problem at all. My mother would love it."

Ben's eyes twinkled when he grinned, and James said, "What?"

Ben tossed his head back and barked out a loud, jovial laugh. "You got it bad, man," he struggled to say when he could catch his breath.

James looked at his hands in his lap, then grinned as he looked up. "Maybe I do. Wouldn't be so bad, would it? But I'm not at all sure she's ready."

"She'll get there. Might be sooner than you think. Seems like women tend to jump in faster than men do." Ben studied James for a moment, then added. "She could do a lot worse, my friend."

"Thanks, Ben. I appreciate that. But I won't push, and I won't marry for less than the right reasons."

"Sounds like a good plan. Why don't you see if she'll accompany you tomorrow then, but if she won't, let me know and I'll change my plans."

"Alright, I will. But I doubt you'll be hearing from me." James smiled and winked, causing Ben to burst into laughter again.

***

James couldn't keep the smile from forming on his face as he walked down the street to Olivia's house. She just had to agree to going with him tomorrow. He would have a hard time accepting her refusal, so he wanted to make sure his invitation was worded in a way she couldn't refuse. He needed to be careful not to make it seem like he was asking for his own sake. It had to be about her safety; the fact that most of the town would be at his parent's plantation all day would leave her and the children vulnerable, and he couldn't accept that.

"Mister MacKay! Did you come to play catch?" Michael leaped off the porch and raced to him, hopping up and down in his excitement.

"Hey, there, little man! Sure, we can play some, if it's okay with your mother. Is she inside?"

Just then, Olivia came out the front door. It looked like she was about to scold Michael's exuberance when James lifted the boy and tossed him up onto his shoulder. Michael's squeal preceded his giggles, and his mother's face turned from serious to amused. James smiled at her, then pretended he was dropping Michael on his head, which caused a startled scream and more giggles.

After a few more minutes, James set Michael down, and the child took a few steps back and charged at James, attempting to tackle him. Playing along, James allowed himself to be knocked to the ground where a wrestling match ensued. They rolled and tumbled and laughed and shouted, all the while having a fun time together.

James looked up to the porch and found Olivia covering her laughter. Even Frannie had abandoned the ever-present book to come outside to see what all the noise was about, and she was laughing, too. Olivia put an arm around Frannie, and the girl leaned into her mother. It was a touching scene.

Eventually, James pretended to be exhausted and beaten, so the roughhousing dwindled. Michael was reluctant to stop completely, and James fended him off with periodic tickling. Michael called for Frannie to come play too, but James was not surprised that she refused. He made a mental note to seek her out and try to connect with her over her books later.

Finally, Olivia called to Michael and asked him if he had completed the chores he was assigned for the afternoon. Reluctantly, the youngster returned to the job he had to finish, leaving James free to talk to Olivia about the next day. Before he had a chance to speak, she invited him to join her on the porch and asked Frannie to bring them each a glass of lemonade.

"What brings you by this afternoon?"

James studied her for a moment before answering. He still had not decided how to approach the invitation to the wedding without it sounding like he was asking to court her. He had decided somewhere between Ben's office that morning and now that he would very much like to do just that, but he wanted to be sure she was willing for their friendship to move in that direction. The last thing he wanted was to frighten her away and perhaps lose the opportunity for them to become a family.

Stifling a smile, he looked out toward the street, checking to see where the deputy might be, then looked back at her.

"I spoke to Ben this morning. There has not been one sign of the bandits all week."

"I assumed that was the case. It seems I would have heard about it if they had been around here. I'm sure they have given up and won't be coming back. Maybe you should just tell them to stop wasting their time." Just then, Frannie returned with two glasses filled with fresh lemonade and a plate of cookies.

Frowning, James replied, "I don't think they've given up. That's not how they operate." Then, smiling at Frannie, James said, "Thank you, Miss Martin. You are a wonderful hostess. This looks delicious. Did you make the cookies?"

Smiling shyly, she glanced at her mother, then back at James. "I helped. These are my favorites. I hope you like them."

"I know I will!" He winked at her, then asked, "So, Frannie, what are you reading about lately? I rarely see you without a book in your hands."

Frannie rolled her eyes. "<u>Robinson Crusoe</u>. Again. I've already read it so many times. But," and her eyes took on a sparkle he'd not seen before. "My dear friend, Naomi, has a book called <u>First Impressions</u> and she's promised that I can borrow it as soon as she's finished with it. I'm so excited! I can't wait to read something new!" She clapped her hands and bounced up and down on her toes. James caught Olivia covering a grin and couldn't help but smile at the girl.

"That sounds wonderful. I'm glad you have such a generous friend. I have a niece named Naomi who is just about your age. What is your friend's last name?"

"Baker. Her father is the best doctor in town," Frannie grinned.

James tried to hide his reaction, then said, "Would you believe she's my niece? Her mama is my sister."

"Really? That's amazing! Her aunt is getting married tomorrow. She asked me to come with her, but Mama said no."

James glanced over at Olivia, who was looking slightly embarrassed. "Frannie, dear, you don't just show up at someone's wedding, or any other party, unless you are invited by the hostess. It's not proper."

James couldn't believe his luck. The perfect opportunity for him to insist they go with him had just fallen into his lap. "As the one officiating the ceremony, and as the big brother of the bride, you are all officially invited. In fact, I insist that you all come with me. It will be fun. I think you all deserve to have a little fun for a day. What do you say, Olivia? Just see how much it would mean to Frannie here. She's about ready to burst with excitement. We can't let that happen, can we?"

Olivia was shaking her head. He needed to find more ways to charm her. This was too important, and he couldn't fail now. Not when the opportunity came so easily.

"Please, Mama? It would mean so much to Naomi!"

James's grin was quick, and he, too, looked at Olivia, one eyebrow quirked as if to say, *"Come on, you don't stand a chance and you know it."* Instead, he said, "My family would love to have you all come. Besides, most of the town will be there anyway. Emily Rose made sure of that. I'm surprised she didn't walk up and down every street in town hand-delivering invitations to every single person."

"I don't know. Let me think about it, and we will discuss it later, Frannie. Now, please go make sure your chores are finished before dinner. It will be ready soon."

The young lady scampered away, skipping and chanting a happy tune. Olivia smiled, shaking her head.

"Actually, I was coming here to invite you to go to the wedding with me anyway. Now you have an even bigger reason to accept. And if those two things are not enough, I wanted to tell you more of what Ben and I discussed out of earshot of the children."

Alarm flared in Olivia's eyes. "Then let's take a walk, just in case they are close by." She peeked inside, then they walked around to the back of the house.

Quietly, James told Olivia about how the sheriff said since there had been no contact made by the bandits, he would not be able to justify keeping the men on guard duty around the clock. He told her how he was certain they had been tipped off that the law was aware of their activities and that's why they hadn't been back to harass her. He emphasized how he wasn't happy about Ben pulling the guards off, but there was nothing he could do about it.

"I'm very uncomfortable leaving you three here in town while most of the rest of town will be at the plantation. I was serious about wanting you to come with me, partially for your own protection, and partially for my own selfish reasons. A bonus is Frannie's close friendship with Naomi. How can you say no?"

Olivia regarded him with a mix of skepticism and amusement. "I guess I should ask what your own selfish reasons are."

Over the past couple of weeks, he had found reasons to come check on them. One morning, he brought the saw he had borrowed from the plantation and cut the branch that threatened the back window. They talked about everything and nothing, and had even discussed building a treehouse for Michael. James no longer refused to acknowledge his growing feelings for this family, particularly the beautiful woman before him.

All signs of teasing melted away as he looked into her eyes. "Because I want to spend time with you. I enjoy your company." *And because I have feelings for you!*

Her eyes searched his face. He saw the moment she realized he was speaking the truth and that it went deeper than that. Her face relaxed, and she sighed in resignation. Still meeting his gaze, she called, "Frannie, please set an extra place at the table. Mister MacKay is joining us for dinner tonight."

Chapter Fourteen

The morning of the wedding dawned bright and clear. It was going to be a beautiful day. James couldn't help the smile that kept creeping onto his face as he shaved and dressed for the day. Not only was he excited to be with his whole family again to celebrate their little sister's wedding, but he would have a beautiful lady and two incredibly fun kids by his side.

Last night had been the best he'd had in - well, in as long as he could remember. He had laughed more than should be proper, and in spite of his efforts to keep it reined in so that he didn't frighten Olivia, she seemed to be having a good time as well. He had teased each of the children and laughed at their antics. Michael kept them entertained by laughing at his own made-up jokes, and Frannie's idea of marriage and romance had them sharing hidden smiles when they caught each other's eye.

Olivia was an excellent cook, if dinner was anything to go on. She had roasted a chicken to a beautiful, golden brown, and her mashed potatoes didn't have a single lump. A fresh spinach salad had been topped with buttermilk dressing, and a corn casserole made his mouth water even now as he thought about it. Light, fluffy biscuits topped with fresh butter and last summer's blackberry jam made him feel like he was eating in a grand, city restaurant. When he complimented her, her cheeks had flamed red as she shyly met his eyes. Her reaction made him vow to take her berry picking at the plantation as soon as the fruit was ripe.

What would it be like to eat like that every day? Victoria had just been getting the hang of cooking for them when she died, and other than his mother, Cookie, and Mrs. Fields, he had not had the opportunity to get used to someone else's cooking, but he could get used to this. It wasn't like she had planned on cooking for him since his invitation had come just before she served it, so apparently, she fed her children well every day.

When he was ready to go, he walked down to the Martin house. Since he hadn't had a chance to borrow a carriage from the plantation, they had decided to use Olivia's wagon. He went around to the stable and found that her horse was already hitched up and ready to go. Michael came bouncing out the back door to greet him.

"Hello, Mister MacKay! I got Muffin ready for us. Mama said I could let you do it, but I wanted to help. I even packed her a feedbag for while we're there in case we're gone too long. She shouldn't miss her lunch on account of a silly old wedding."

James didn't even try to hide his smile. "No, she shouldn't, you're absolutely right, Michael. I appreciate you taking care of all this. You're getting to be quite the man, aren't you?"

"Mama says if I keep it up, she'll give me more things to be 'sponsible for. Maybe she'll even let me have a treehouse. Say, Mister MacKay, do you know how to build stuff? Can you show me how to build a treehouse?"

"Well, now, Michael, we would have to talk to your Mama about that. If she were to agree, I'm sure I can teach you a few things." Michael whooped and cheered. "But only if she says it's okay."

"I know. I think she'll say yes. Do you have tools? Do you know how to cut wood? We'll need nails. Can we put it in the tree by my bedroom window so I can climb in and out? That would be so much fun. I can camp out in it. Mister MacKay, do you know how to camp out? You wanna camp out with me?"

Finally, the boy seemed to run out of questions, at least for the moment. James laughed. "How about if we just take it one step at a time, alright? We can figure it all out as we go along. The first and most important thing we have to do is make sure your mother approves of the idea. We can't do anything without her permission, understand?"

"What do you need my permission for?"

James turned to answer her, but the vision he saw made his mouth dry up and his tongue stick to his teeth. She was stunning. Fortunately, he didn't have to form words because Michael answered her in his exuberant, bouncy way. After listening to Michael, she looked up at him and her smile fell away.

Self-consciously, she looked down at her dress and put her hand near her throat. "Is - is this dress okay for today? I wasn't sure what to wear."

James had to clear his throat twice before he could make a sound. "It's more than okay. You're beautiful." He spoke the words while looking into her eyes. Yes, the dress was lovely, but the woman looked amazing. Her honey blond hair was piled on top of her head in an elegant twist, and the blue silk gown that matched the color of her eyes hugged her figure in all the right places. Over her arm, she carried a white lacy shawl and a small, white reticule with lace trim.

"Thank you," she replied quietly. Then, as though making an effort to remove the attention from herself, she added with a grin, "You clean up pretty well yourself, Mister MacKay."

James snapped out of the trance he had been in and grinned back at her. "Where's Frannie? Are you all ready to go? Looks like this is going to be a beautiful day." Michael clambered aboard the wagon, and James handed Olivia up to her seat just as Frannie ran out the door and climbed in next to Michael.

***

When James turned the team into the lane leading to the plantation, nerves in the shape of butterflies attacked Olivia's stomach. They had spent enough time together this past week that she was comfortable with him and shouldn't be nervous, but never before had she gone anywhere with a man who was not her husband. Not only was this an outing that most people attend with family, it was an outing with James's *whole* family, people she knew, but not in connection with James.

What might they think of her showing up with him like this?

James seemed to sense her tension and glanced over at her. His arm twitched, like he was considering reaching over to touch her and perhaps take her hand. Her cheeks flamed at the idea, but surprisingly, she didn't dislike it. Still, for the sake of her children and people who would be observing them, she was glad he did not touch her.

"Are you nervous? You seem a little tense," his question was quiet, for her ears only.

She smiled up at him. "I suppose I am a little nervous. We weren't exactly invited, so that feels awkward."

"But you know a lot of these people. No one will think anything of it."

"Except that I'm coming with you, and that makes it seem like a big deal."

"If it makes you feel better, I've explained to my parents what happened with the bandits, so they will be happy you're here where you are safe. Besides, I know that you and the children are friends with some of my family members. They will just assume that since we live near each other, we simply came together. Efficiency, you know." James smiled and winked at her. "And, just in case the bandits are in the area, I'll ask my brothers and a few people I trust to help keep an eye on things. Above all, I want you all to be safe."

Without thinking, she laid her hand on his arm and squeezed gently. "Thank you, James. I can't tell you how much it means that you are going out of your way to help me like this."

James's eyes darkened. "It's my pleasure, Olivia."

Suddenly, it seemed that there were children everywhere. Frannie and Michael couldn't wait to get out of the wagon to run off with their friends who had noticed their arrival. James set the brake, then stepped down and went around the wagon to help Olivia while one of the stable hands came and took the horse and wagon to the appointed place.

James seemed reluctant to release her, but his family was closing in fast. Olivia stepped away from him with a look that seemed to shake him out of his trance. After a quick smile in her direction, he turned to greet his brothers.

"Olivia, I'm sure you know some of these scoundrels, particularly this one," he grinned as he pounded Edward on the back in a half hug. "And this is Charles, and this one is Colin, also known as Deputy MacKay. And this guy I'm sure you know, Doc John Baker, or Naomi's dad, is married to my sister Ellie," he exchanged a grin with her. "David is my sister Savannah's husband, and this is Jacob, who says he's brave enough to marry into our family today." They all laughed as James affectionately squeezed the young man's shoulder. Then, he quietly continued. "Gentlemen, Olivia Martin is my neighbor, and I hope you'll not ask too many questions, but we could use your help in keeping an eye on her and her children today. There has been some trouble in town, which is why she agreed to accompany me here today."

Olivia twisted her fingers, then lifted her chin and met each man's eyes. "I'm pleased to meet all of you. Thank you for allowing my children and I to attend your festivities uninvited today."

"If James invited you, you were invited. Enough said." She couldn't remember which of the men responded, but she sent him a grateful smile.

"I'd like to introduce you to my parents before we all get pulled in different directions shortly. Are you ready?" James offered his arm, and she nodded and took it, allowing him to lead her away.

Her neck warmed, wondering what the men they had just been with might be thinking now. She didn't know if it was common for James to bring a woman to family events or not, but all of them had the good grace to take her presence in stride. Evidently, James had enough clout as the eldest brother to command unquestioned respect. She was surprised to realize how much that quality held a certain attraction for her.

Her life with Peter had been one that garnered respect from most people. He was a hard worker and a solid Christian man, and the way he treated her in public was the way he treated her at home. Her life had been sheltered in that regard, and maybe she took it for granted. He was affectionate but respectful, kind but decisive. Was he perfect? No, no one was, but she realized he had been perfect for her. And until that moment, she had believed that Peter would always be the only man who would ever love her, because she would never settle for anything less than how he had made her feel.

Until this mess with the bandits, she naively thought that most women were treated well, but those men had frightened her more than she wanted to admit. What would she have done without the help of James, and the sheriff and his deputies? Would she have fallen prey to the bandits? Abandoned the home Peter built for them? Where would they have gone? She didn't have any family to turn to.

James seemed to be the kind of man she would be content to settle down with if she ever decided to marry again. She knew that it was usually expected of widows to remarry so that they were taken care of by someone and didn't become the responsibility of the community, but to her way of thinking, it was still too soon. Besides, Zeke, Peter's foreman who had taken over the construction company after his death, had set up a trust fund that the company continued to pay into to provide for her and the children. They should not ever want for anything.

Her mind wandered to the interactions she and James had had over the past couple of weeks. He had seemed to enjoy playing with Michael and having literary discussions with Frannie. And she had enjoyed watching them come alive under his attention. While she still mourned her husband's death, she was grateful to James for helping her children find some normalcy in the midst of their grief.

She felt his hand cover hers on his arm and was startled to realize they had stopped walking and were standing in front of a handsome older man. James was introducing her to the man as his father, Henry MacKay. Pink tinged her cheeks when she realized she had been lost in her thoughts of *him* and nearly missed the introduction! James gave her a curious look, but his eyes twinkled with mirth as though he knew what she had been thinking. She grinned and shook her head slightly, then turned to answer a question from Mister MacKay.

A sharp tug on her sleeve alerted her that her daughter had arrived at her side and insisted on gaining her attention. She turned her attention to Frannie momentarily and found that Naomi and her mother, Ellie, were also coming toward them.

"Mama, is it alright if I go with Naomi to see the kittens in the barn? Please?" The young girl was bouncing up and down on her toes, excited to play with the little fluffballs.

"I'll make sure she doesn't get lost, Missus Martin. Please?" Naomi drew out her dramatic request.

"Well, I don't know," Olivia started, looking over their heads to learn Ellie's opinion on the subject.

"They will be just fine, I assure you. I can't promise they won't get a little dusty up there in the loft, however." Ellie laughed and waved a hand, the gesture showing she admitted that trying to keep children clean was a losing battle. She was right, although Olivia had found that Frannie was the easy one. Michael was the one who needed a bath nearly every night.

"Try not to get too dirty, alright? It's still early, and not even time for the wedding yet."

"Thank you, Mama! I'll be careful!" Ellie and Olivia shared a laugh, and the young girls scampered off toward the barn.

"I'm so glad to see you here today. Naomi is thrilled that you decided to let Frannie come to the wedding. She has been wanting to show her around the plantation for a while now."

"We would not have come if James had not insisted."

Ellie's eyebrows shot to the edge of her bonnet.

"You came with James? That's wonderful." She smiled at Olivia, who suddenly looked flustered. "He's a great guy, even if he is my big brother."

"He's been very kind. I went to him for legal advice when he first hung his shingle at the end of my street. The timing was excellent." Olivia was reluctant to divulge too much information, even though she felt certain she could trust any of James's family. Still, she wasn't sure if she should say more.

Ellie hooked her arm through Olivia's. "Well, I'm glad he brought you. I've been needing a reason to get better acquainted with you. After all, our girls are the best of friends, and as summer comes, I'm sure they will create reasons to be together more frequently." She laughed with amusement, and Olivia couldn't help but join her. "There are much worse places for children to play and grow than here at the plantation. Frannie is welcome here anytime. Michael, too."

"Thank you. We appreciate that. I'm sure they would love it."

They walked around, Ellie introducing Olivia to everyone they met, and although she was enjoying herself, she found her eyes straying to find James pretty often. Whenever their eyes met, they exchanged smiles.

Sometimes James winked at her, and she realized she missed his closeness. This was a feeling she would need to examine later when she was alone in her room, where children did not interrupt and where twinkling hazel eyes did not seek to invade her thoughts.

Chapter Fifteen

The wedding was beautiful. Emily Rose was a stunning bride, and she amused family and friends alike with her bubbly personality. Olivia enjoyed watching the MacKay family interact with one another and was mesmerized as she watched James in his officiating capacity. He was easy-going and kind, as well as professional, and it was apparent his whole family adored him.

"I'm so glad you came with James today, Olivia," a soft voice spoke behind her left shoulder a fraction of a second before a warm hand touched her arm. Startled, she turned to find James's mother, Catherine. The matriarch of the MacKay clan wore a twinkle in her eye as though she knew Olivia's thoughts. Her cheeks flushed, and Cathrine chuckled. "Are you enjoying yourself, my dear?"

"Yes, very much. Thank you for having us. I felt awful just barging in like we did, but James assured me it would not be a problem. Is there something I can do to help you?"

"Absolutely not! You are here to enjoy yourself today. We have plenty of help but thank you for offering. Instead, would you like to walk with me for a few minutes? I was just headed to the refreshments for a cool drink."

"Yes, that sounds lovely," Olivia answered, even as she wondered what the older woman had in mind. Did she have something specific she wanted to talk about? Was she going to warn her not to lose her heart to her son? Wait, where did that notion come from? Was Olivia in danger of losing her heart? She didn't think that was possible, in spite of how kind, handsome, and dashing he was. Oh my, the list of his good qualities could go on and on. Olivia drew in a deep breath and let it out slowly.

Catherine hooked an arm through Olivia's. *This must be a family trait*, Olivia thought, amused, and she smiled to herself. As they walked, she cast a searching eye toward the last place she had seen James. He was walking toward them with his father, and he winked when his eyes met hers. Belatedly, she realized Catherine had asked her a question.

"I'm so sorry. My mind had wandered, and I didn't hear your question. Would you mind repeating it?"

Catherine's smile lit her face, and her eyes twinkled merrily, turning Olivia's face red. She wished she could blame a hot sun for her red face, but the truth was, the weather was mild, even if it was beautiful. No, can't blame the sun.

"James told us about the trouble you've had in town, and I was wondering if you have been bothered by the bandits recently."

"Oh. No, actually, they have not been back, and none of the deputies have seen them around town, either. I'm hoping they gave up on trying to steal my house, but James doesn't seem to think that is the case.

I'm so grateful for the men giving up their time to guard our home. The whole thing has been quite frightening."

"I'm sure it has. I'm glad James lives so close to you. He's a good man. You can count on him anytime, you know."

"Yes, he's been very kind to us. My children certainly enjoy it whenever he comes around. He discusses literature with Frannie and plays with Michael. I appreciate that. They're missing their father."

Catherine squeezed her arm gently. "I know they are. I have not experienced loss like you have, but I'm sure it's been hard for all of you. I want you to know you have an open invitation to come here anytime you'd like. And if there is ever a time you are afraid in your house, come stay with us, alright?"

Olivia fought tears that threatened to fall. "Thank you, Missus MacKay. You are so kind."

"Please, call me Catherine." She reached an arm around Olivia's shoulder and gave it an affectionate squeeze.

"Thank you, Catherine." The ladies smiled at each other as they reached the refreshment table. The men arrived there just a couple of steps ahead of them.

James took two glasses and handed one to Olivia. "What are you two conspiring about?" he asked with a smile.

"Nothing for you to be concerned about, Son. We were just getting better acquainted, weren't we, Olivia?"

"That's right." She took a sip of lemonade to avoid having to answer further, but she felt James's eyes on her.

"I think the musicians will be starting soon. May I have the first dance, Olivia?"

"Of course. But first I should check on the children."

James laughed. "Last I knew, Michael was throwing a ball with the other boys, and Frannie and Naomi were carrying kittens around like they were babies. Those poor kittens won't remember what their jobs are when those two get through with them." Everyone laughed.

"I remember someone else as a young lad doing the same thing. Ye heard the wee things raisin' a fuss and was certain their mum had abandoned them. We had quite a time convincin' ye to take 'em back to the barn." Henry shook his head as he laughed.

Olivia laughed at James's look of mock outrage. "I never did such a thing!" His eyes crinkled at the corners when he smiled at her. Goodness, the man had a nice smile!

After bidding farewell to his parents, James and Olivia went in search of the children, if for no other reason than to put her mind at ease. James was discovering that he'd be willing to do almost anything for her. And, he realized that thought didn't bother him in the least. But he should be careful not to scare her away. He wanted to make sure she was ready to jump into another relationship and not feel pressured. He'd let her take some of the lead in their relationship, see what she was thinking.

Just as he had predicted, Michael was playing ball with some of the boys near the orchard. They stopped to watch just in time to hear Michael telling the boys that his neighbor, Mister MacKay, had been playing catch with him and teaching him some ball handling skills. They smiled at each other, knowing he was doing just fine on his own, and James chuckled since several of those boys were his nephews.

Next, they found Frannie and Naomi surrounded by a group of children of varying sizes. James enjoyed watching the light play over Olivia's face as she watched her daughter. She was such a lovely woman, and he found himself wanting to lead her away from all other eyes for a chance to… what, hold her? Kiss her? Would she even consider allowing that? No, better stick with the plan and allow her to lead them just a bit.

Maybe it was the event of the day that had his emotions in a tangle. He wasn't sure, but he knew the last time he felt like this about a woman was just before he asked Victoria to be his wife. The difference was,

Victoria wasn't still mourning her husband. James clenched his fists, reminding himself to take it slow.

It wasn't that God was using Olivia as bait, dangling her in front of him to see what he would do with the temptation. No, he knew God didn't behave that way. He thought it was entirely possible she was the woman God had brought into his life. After all, he had told the Lord he thought he was ready, and if He wanted him to have someone to spend the rest of his life with, he was open to it. So, why wouldn't He answer this way, literally placing her in his path? It seemed entirely likely.

As they walked, they stopped briefly, speaking to different clusters of friends and neighbors along the way. Most of them, James knew, and he spent a few moments getting reacquainted, introducing them to Olivia if they didn't already know one another. He was enjoying having her on his arm, and the inquisitive looks some folks sent his way didn't bother him like it would have in the past. If people wanted to speculate, he wasn't going to stop them.

Soon enough, the music began, and he led her to where the dancing was to be held on the veranda. A thrill shot through him as he anticipated holding her in his arms while they danced.

Leaning down, he whispered in her ear, "Is it too presumptuous of me to want to fill your dance card with my name?"

Olivia's soft look was followed by one of amusement. "You might want to save that thought in case I trample on your toes until you can't walk," she giggled, and he decided she was the most adorable thing he had ever seen. *Okay, Lord, how long will you make me wait?*

***

James's question nearly threw Olivia off balance, and she scrambled to add some humor to keep from melting into a puddle. James was just adorable. However, if she was to move forward in a relationship with him, more than the friendship they already had, she needed to be sure. But when he said things like that in her ear, her heart was in jeopardy of flying right out of her chest and into his very capable hands.

Oh my! How was she ever going to be sure about this man? His whole family had welcomed her and the children with open arms, not questioning either of them at all. She thought they were probably thrilled that he was finally showing interest in someone after fifteen long years. Olivia was sure they had probably been worried about him. It was evident he was well loved by all of them.

But what did they think about her? It had only been a few months since Peter's death. Surely, they must think it was too soon, right? And yet, his mother had invited her to come to the plantation anytime she wanted to. Did that mean with or without James? She thought it would feel awkward to come without him, but if she came with him, how would that appear? Would it tie them together in the minds of everyone else?

Maybe not. They all seemed like a reasonable bunch of people. Surely, the two of them could be friendly without being lumped together in a relationship they didn't want. But what if they *did* both want it? She thought back to what James had told her the previous night. *"Because I want to spend time with you. I enjoy your company."* It had appeared there was more he wanted to say but didn't. It made her curious.

They stepped onto the dance floor and James drew her into his arms. She had a flash of memory of Peter doing the same thing. Would she be able to see James and not Peter if she allowed the relationship to flourish? She risked a glance upward and caught her breath when their eyes met. No, this man definitely was not Peter.

She had been very much in love with Peter and had been excited to grow old with that man. He was handsome and fun, loving and kind, and she knew he cherished her always. She had been convinced that no other man would ever make her feel that way again.

And yet, the way James looked at her, his hazel eyes gazing into hers, then tracing the features of her face as though memorizing them, made her doubt her previous conviction. As she returned his gaze, her thoughts wavered.

He tugged her a little bit closer. "You're so beautiful, Olivia."

She sucked in a breath, catching her bottom lip in her teeth. "Thank you, James." Her voice sounded so breathy, so soft. How he affected her! Maybe she should ask him what else he had wanted to say to her the night before. Was she that bold?

Before she could form the words, he spoke again. "I keep reminding myself that I need to give you plenty of time, but I think I should tell you a little bit more about my feelings." Her eyes searched his face as he continued. "I want you to know that just before we met, I had a talk with the Lord, and I told Him that if He had someone for me, that I wouldn't be opposed. Olivia, I was attracted to you immediately, but then I've had many years to recover from losing my family, and it is still pretty new for you. My feeling is that He brought us together, but I'm willing to wait as long as you need me to."

Olivia caught her breath. She was afraid to blink for fear the pools that had formed in her eyes would spill out and run down her face. Slowly, she began to put her thoughts into words. "If I were to re-marry, he would have to know my children well, and they would have to approve of him."

"I know them. And they seem to like me just fine." He grinned.

One side of her mouth tugged up in response to him. "Yes, but you would not want to take on two half-grown children."

James leaned in, touching his forehead to hers. "Darlin', why don't you let me decide that. Unless you're saying YOU are not interested in me..."

She stammered, looking around at the people dancing near them and everywhere but at him. Then, meeting his eyes, she said, "I'm not saying I wouldn't be interested, but we are a lot. The children might have trouble accepting a new father."

Holding her securely to him, he looked into her eyes. "Olivia, I would never want to take the place of their father. I want to support you in helping them remember him. And I want to help you continue being the best mother any child could ever have. You are wonderful with them, and I would never want to be in the way of your relationship with them.

He continued to look into her eyes, never wavering, watching different emotions flit across her face. Some looked like hope, others resembled despair. The song came to an end, and James realized there was more that needed to be said. "Let's go take a walk. There's a nice cool path in the grove of trees right over there."

She nodded and allowed him to lead the way, her arm securely tucked in his. They managed to escape the press of guests and made their way to the path James had mentioned. She was aware of the warring emotions, each trying to take up residence in her mind. She struggled to keep her tears at bay, but she knew that with James, it wouldn't matter. She knew he would understand, and that he would want to help her through this riot of emotions that kept trying to control her.

When they were far away from other people, James took a deep breath and guided her to take a seat on a bench. He crouched down and gripped both her shoulders in his hands, his thumbs moving up and down on her upper arms. "Olivia, I have come to care for you deeply already. In fact, I'm falling in love with you."

Her eyes snapped to his. "You don't want to love me. I'm sure there is a much more deserving woman somewhere. You're a good man, James, and I appreciate your friendship and everything you've done for my children and me, but you could do so much better than me.

He tilted his head to the side, studying her for a moment. "You have a pretty low opinion of yourself. What happened to cause that?"

"I'm just not worthy. Of anyone or anything good."

"Peter loved you. Are you saying you were not worthy of his love either?"

Her eyes studied the ground. "Exactly, because now I'm being punished."

James's eyebrows drew in toward the middle. "Why do you think you're being punished?" he asked, genuinely confused.

"Don't you see? Everyone I love has been taken. I'm afraid something bad will happen to one or both of my children. Maybe I didn't love Peter enough. Maybe there are things I should have done differently. He made me feel cherished, but I wonder if he felt cherished, too. I wonder if he was disappointed in me, but he was just too kind to say it. There are times I should have made his favorite meal or dessert, or gone on an adventure with him, but there was always an excuse, or it was easy to put off for "the next time". But now there will be no "next time". I let him down, so now I'm being punished. I'm not worthy of love, so God punishes me."

James watched quietly while she twisted her fingers in her lap, then leaned forward, forearms on his thighs. "Listen to me, Olivia. Bad things happen to good people all the time. That does not mean we deserve the bad things that happen. God uses the things He allows to happen, not because he's punishing us, but to help us grow closer to Him. That's what he wants most because He loves us. He loves *you*." She looked away, anguish etched on her face. "Look at me" He gently took her hands in his. "God. Loves. You. YOU, Olivia Martin."

"I know that in my head, but I have a hard time feeling it. I confess my unbelief all the time, but something inside me just doesn't accept it. I don't know how to change that." The tears that had been threatening began to fall.

"You know, Satan thrives on making us believe his lies. Sometimes people say things that hurt us, not because they mean to, but Satan uses their words to reinforce the bad feelings we have about ourselves. But, stop believing the lies, because things happen. People die. Kids get sick. Houses are destroyed. All sorts of things happen. You know how I know these things?"

Shyly, Olivia looked at him. "I know I'm not the only one. Bad things happened to you too."

"Yes. But I also know because I believe every word in the Bible is true. There are a few verses that have helped me through a lot of the same doubt you're facing right now. Paul teaches us in Romans chapter eight verse thirty-five, 'Who shall separate us from the love of Christ? Shall tribulation, or distress, or persecution, or famine, or nakedness, or peril, or sword?' Then a few verses later, it says, 'Nay, in all these things we are more than conquerors through Him that loved us. For I am persuaded that neither death, nor life, nor angels, nor principalities, nor powers, nor things present, nor things to come, nor height, nor depth, nor any other creature, shall be able to separate us from the love of God, which is in Christ Jesus our Lord.' See, that's a lot of stuff, everything you can imagine that's bad, but it cannot stop God from loving YOU. So even if we never catch these guys who are trying to steal your house and worry you, it's not because you did anything wrong. Your parents' deaths were not because you did wrong. Peter's tragic accident was not because you did anything wrong. God uses these kinds of things to bring us closer to him. I know it's hard to accept when we're going through those hard things. I've been there. I completely understand. And I'll be here to help you through it, every step. I know you are loveable because God loves you. Let Him use me to show you what His love is like. When you understand His love, you will be able to love yourself and maybe then you'll know what I see in you, too." As her tears fell, he slid onto the bench beside her and gathered her up, bringing her closer to his side and tucking her head under his chin. He sat there holding her tenderly and kissing the top of her head, stroking her arm while she wept into his chest.

Chapter Sixteen

Early the next day, Ben came into James's office. He pulled up a chair, took off his hat, and rubbed the back of his neck.

"What's going on, my friend?"

"I didn't want to bother you with this last night since I know you were gone most of the day for your sister's wedding. Wouldn't have mattered anyway. I went out to Reicher's place like we talked about. The man was nowhere to be found. Place was abandoned. No livestock, nothin'. I searched around a bit, and it looked like only horses had been in the corral and stables, no other animals at all. Then I stopped at the land office and found out that property has been owned by Thompsons for decades. Not sure how that slipped by me when vetting him for deputy, but it just indicates to me that they're a slippery bunch, up to no good. Could be the guy's name isn't even Reicher. So, I'm gonna go out on a limb here and say your hunch was dead on. That guy was a spy for the bandits."

"Darn. I was hoping I was wrong."

"Me, too. I can't believe I was so bamboozled by his logical questions and smooth answers before I deputized him." Ben shook his head and clenched his fists.

"Well, don't beat yourself up about it. We'll find 'em, but now they know we're onto them and they'll probably flee the area. Let's check with other towns, see if there have been more incidents."

"I'm one step ahead of you. I sent telegrams to a few other sheriffs this morning before I came here. Here's a list of the ones I contacted. Figured you'd want to check in with your guys, too. I just told 'em to be on the lookout for a guy fitting his description, probably with several other men, unknown number, and that we suspect them preying on widows."

"I know of a few of these men. I'll go send out my notices, too. Maybe we'll get something back soon. Meanwhile, I won't let up my guard on Olivia. In fact,

I aim to convince her to come here during the day when they're most likely to approach her."

Ben grinned. "What excuse are you giving her for coming here during the day?"

James chuckled. "What makes you think I need an excuse?" Ben barked out a laugh. "Actually, I was thinking of asking her to come to work for me. I could use some help organizing files and such. I was going to hire a lady anyway, why not her? Two-fold purpose. I get the office help I need, and I get to spend time with her every day," James excused with a grin, as if his logic made all the sense in the world.

Ben rose to his feet, continuing to laugh. "I wish you lots of luck, if that's what you're aimin' for. But don't forget the most important part. She gets the protection she needs."

James sobered. "You're right, of course. We laugh, but her safety is more important to me than my need for office help. I'll send my messages and talk to her. Let me know if you hear anything, and I'll do the same."

"See ya 'round, James."

After Ben left, James sat back in his desk chair thinking about the conversation. How had they missed this before? Why hadn't he mentioned his suspicions to Ben sooner, as he had intended to do? Maybe they could have caught Reicher before he left town.

James made a fist and pounded it on his desk. Where had the man gone? Did he disappear back into the hills with his gang? Were they still going to prey on widows of this area, or would they move on to a farther away region full of unsuspecting souls?

If they weren't caught, how many more poor ladies would fall victim to their underhanded activities? They still didn't know the gang's motive. And, God forbid, would they become more violent now that they were being sought? To his knowledge, so far, the worst thing they had done was frighten widows. He hoped they didn't become desperate enough to do something horrible.

James grabbed his hat and locked the office. There was no better time to talk to Olivia than now, while the children were at school. In spite of the problem still hanging over them, he walked with a bounce in his step in anticipation of seeing her this morning.

As he approached her front door, a scream ripped through the air. At first it was loud and shrill, but was quickly reduced to a muffled whimper, and it sounded like it was coming from the back of the house. Panic gripped James, and the smile that had been hovering around his mouth crashed to the ground.

The bandits! Had they slipped past him and infiltrated the neighborhood from behind the row of houses? If they had, what were they doing to Olivia? Was it one or more of the men? He would never forgive himself for not staying closer if they hurt her.

His mind stopped working and his heart took over. Leaping onto the porch, he didn't even hesitate to announce his presence. He pulled the door open with a force that would have pulled less sound construction from its hinges and darted through the parlor toward where he had heard the scream.

He forced himself to slow down, planning to use the element of surprise to his advantage. Leaning against the wall, he peered around the portal into the kitchen. He hadn't heard any voices, and that puzzled him, but he didn't take the time to try and figure it out. What he found was not at all what he was expecting.

Olivia was standing on a chair, frying pan in her hand, one foot resting on the edge of the table as though ready to climb. James did a quick check around the room to see who or what might have frightened her. On the other side of the room, oblivious to its imminent demise, was a baby raccoon.

Mirth bubbled up his throat and threatened to spill out. He must have made a sound, because Olivia suddenly spun around, raising her skillet above her head, holding on with both hands, fright in her eyes. And then, everything happened in slow motion.

The quick spin on the chair must have sent her off balance, because the next thing James knew, she was screaming again while toppling through the air. His fast reflexes put wings on his feet, and he flew to the table, catching her just as she came off the chair. The impact of landing in his arms caused her raised hands to come down hard, bringing the skillet with them, knocking him on the head.

They both landed with a thud. Somehow, James had managed to get his body underneath her to cushion the fall. When they both caught their breath, they spoke at the same time.

"Are you hurt?"

"Are you okay?"

Then James began to laugh. Olivia struggled to sit up next to him and scooted away, just watching him for a moment.

"What are you doing? Why are you in my house?"

"I heard you scream."

"From down the street?" Her huge eyes and incredulous tone set him off again into more fits of laughter. "What is so funny, Mister MacKay?"

Twinkling eyes looked into hers as he struggled to control the humor. "Oh, I guess I'm in trouble now. You called me 'Mister MacKay'."

One quirked eyebrow was his answer, and he chuckled again, then sat up.

"I was coming here to talk to you, and just as I approached the door to knock, I heard you scream. All rational thought left me. I was only concerned for your safety." James looked around the room, apparently trying to locate the perpetrator that had caused all the trouble. "I expected to find a human bandit accosting you rather than a little furry one. I suppose my relief was so great that it made me laugh. I am sorry for startling you and causing you to fall from your perch. Are you sure you are not hurt?"

Both her eyebrows lifted briefly. It was evident that she was struggling not to give in to her own laughter from the twitching at the corners of her mouth. Then she shook her head. "No, I'm fine, now that my heart has settled back into my chest where it belongs."

James's eyes roamed her face, settling on her lips. Briefly, he wished he had the liberty to comfort her in his arms, kissing her until her heart raced back out of her chest. Instead, he got to his feet and offered her a hand, helping her to hers.

"What were you planning to do with the skillet? Bop that thing on the head or catch it and cook it?" He grinned as she smacked him in the stomach with the skillet. Man, this lady was fun to tease.

"No, but if you want to catch it, I'll cook it and feed it to you." James could no longer control the laughter, but to his delight, she joined him, then walked over to the cabinet and put the pan away.

"I had the door open for some fresh air. The poor thing must have wandered in while my back was turned. I saw movement out of the corner of my eye and just grabbed the first thing I could put my hands on. Apparently, I'm more afraid of it than it is of me, because while I was screaming and climbing up on the chair, it sat there looking at me like I was crazy."

"Then I came in and gave you more of a fright." James rubbed the top of his head. "I kinda wish the critter was the one you'd bopped on the head, though."

She covered her mouth, trying to smother a giggle. "I'm so sorry. I didn't mean to hit you, but everything happened so fast, and I couldn't control the motion."

James grinned and winked. "I'm sure I'll recover, especially if you let me join you for dinner tonight."

She rolled her eyes, and he caught a grin as she turned away from him. "I suppose that is an acceptable payment. Especially if it means you don't take me to court for assault." She glanced over her shoulder and grinned at him. Goodness, but she was adorable! "So, what were you coming to talk to me about?"

James walked over to the door and looked out. He saw a baby raccoon, hopefully the same one who had come to visit, scampering into the brush behind the carriage house. Turning back to her, he told her about his visit with Ben earlier.

"I have to admit, hearing you scream earlier terrified me, Olivia. I was afraid you were being attacked by the bandits. We still don't know what their motives are, and now that they've fled the area, it might be harder to catch them. I'm not convinced you are out of danger, and until we know for sure, I'd like to keep you closer to me."

Olivia squinted her eyes in question. "Are you sure this isn't some ploy?"

"Would it be a terrible way to spend your time?" he asked with a hint of teasing in his voice. "Your safety and that of your children comes first, regardless of what my wishes are." He stood in front of her, tucking a loose strand of hair behind her ear, then gathered her hands in his, stroking their backs with his thumbs. "We are still trying to locate those scoundrels, but like I told you yesterday, I care deeply for you, and I can't stand the idea that someone might hurt you."

"I appreciate that, James. But you can't spend all your time here babysitting me. You have a business to run. I'll be fine, especially since I know you are right down the street. Besides, school will be finished soon, and the children will be here as well. I won't be alone."

"Well, I have a solution. I find myself in need of some help around the office. I'd like you to come to work for me during the day. When the children are around, we can find things for them to do also. I have a feeling they could learn a lot from being around the office."

Olivia withdrew her hands from his and walked to the other side of the kitchen. Leaning her hip against the counter top and folding her arms over her chest, she regarded him, considering his suggestion. Because that's what it was, just a suggestion. He could not demand that she do as he asked. He wouldn't. Would he?

"I need to think about this, James. It might not be a good idea for us to spend so much time together."

"Why not? I think it's a perfect solution."

She stammered, trying to find a reason to refuse his request.

"I… uh… well… because."

James grinned, walking toward her. "That doesn't sound like a very convincing argument to me. I'll give you some time to think about it, but will you do something for me while you are thinking?"

She looked at him warily. "Like what?"

"I need to go to the telegraph office and send out some wires to my contacts and get a message to Roger. Come with me so I know you're safe while I'm gone. We can talk while we walk. Ask as many questions as you want. I want you to be completely comfortable with the whole plan, okay?"

"I suppose that would be acceptable."

"Good. Are you ready to go then?"

At her nod, they headed out the door toward town.

Chapter Seventeen

"Watch for small-framed, skittish dark-haired man, known as Aerick Reicher. Believed to be part of bandit group. Increased concern. Fled Jessup. Report anything to Sheriff or myself. James MacKay." James sent the telegram to any contact he could think of from the circuit, including Roger Jefferies. On the chance there would be a response soon, he and Olivia went to the mercantile for a few supplies he needed at his place.

"Is there anything you need while we're here? I'm hoping to hear something back from someone soon, so take your time and get whatever you need."

"There really isn't anything I need, unless you have a specific request for tonight?"

She raised questioning eyebrows at him. He grinned, and she left one brow quirked, causing him to laugh. All the way to the telegraph office, she had voiced concerns over his proposed arrangement, and he countered with reasons he considered valid.

To James, the banter was entertaining, but he sensed that she was beginning to get annoyed with him over it, so he withdrew the tease that was on the tip of his tongue. The last thing he wanted to do was drive her away before he had convinced her to be his. They had been enjoying their time together recently and he didn't want to ruin it with childish behavior. Truth was, he hadn't felt so young in years, and he was having fun, but he still had to keep in mind that she was not finished grieving Peter.

Did one ever completely finish grieving a loved one? Not really. The sharpness of it becomes less painful, but when that person was so significantly part of your life for so long, the loss would always be felt to some extent. He wanted to be the one to help fill the hole left in her heart when she was ready to let him. So, instead of behaving like a child, he said, "Olivia, you don't have to feed me dinner. You are not obligated to do that."

He was unprepared for her reaction. She stopped and stared at him, then turned and walked out the door! What just happened? He started to go after her, then remembered the items he needed to purchase that were still in his hand. He wasn't sure if he should pay now or go after her. He scraped his chin off the floor, laid down the things in his hand, deciding to go after her first and come back later, but by the time he got to the boardwalk in front of the store, she was well on her way back home. He had to run to catch her, zigzagging around the people between them who looked at him with a mixture of annoyance and curiosity.

"Olivia, wait. Olivia!" She increased her speed. Goodness! Was she angry with him? What had he done or said to invoke her ire? When he had almost caught up with her, she turned down a side street, as though in an attempt to keep him from being near her. He reached out and grabbed her arm to stop her. Her glare stunned him.

"What's wrong? Why did you just take off like that?"

Stormy eyes frowned at him as she attempted to yank her arm away from him. "Leave me alone, James. Just let me go." Her eyes glistened, hinting at tears just below the surface.

He was so stunned, he dropped his hand and watched as she stormed away from him. He followed at a distance, wanting to make sure she arrived home safely, and giving her time to calm down. He had no idea what had just happened, and he was determined to find out, but past experience with Victoria and his sisters had taught him that he couldn't push too hard.

There is a fine line between showing a woman you care and proving that you don't. At least in her opinion. James remembered watching as his father had found himself trying to figure out whether he was in trouble for smothering his wife or in trouble because he was oblivious to her needs. James sighed. In his desire to love Olivia, he'd forgotten that it wasn't always rosy.

Now he just had to decide how much time to give her before demanding to know what he had done.

He followed her all the way back to their street, then sat in a chair on his porch while he contemplated what to do next. He had seen her go into her house, so he assumed she was safe, but he wouldn't let this go on very long before going to talk to her. He was certain she wouldn't be coming back to talk to *him* anytime soon. He guessed there was a lot they still needed to work on if they were to have a good relationship. Not if; when. Because it *was* going to happen.

Just then, a messenger arrived to deliver a telegram for him. He paid the lad, then opened the envelope. Glancing at the bottom, he saw it was from Sheriff Matt O'Connor in Orchard Grove.

"Missus Fields broke her leg. Won't let anyone help. Thought you'd like to know. Matt"

The blood drained from James's face, concern for the dear, grandmotherly lady filling his immediate thoughts. He wished there was a faster way to communicate with his friend in Orchard Grove. He wanted more details. Was she in a lot of pain? What of the boarding house? Someone would need to keep it open for her or she'd lose too much money while she was recovering. Unfortunately, he wouldn't be able to do anything about her business, but maybe Matt knew of someone who could help.

It would take more than half a day to drive out there, because if he went, he'd take a wagon and bring her back with him. He got up and paced back and forth on the porch, rubbing the tension in the back of his neck and thinking of a solution to his problems. He was sure he could take her to the plantation. His mother and Cookie would love to dote on her. The problem would be convincing her to leave her home and come with him.

Deciding he needed to send another wire back to Matt right away, he practically ran down the steps and turned toward Olivia's house. First, he needed to let her know that he was going back to town. As he approached her house, he saw that she was in the backyard hanging laundry. She saw him as he came around the corner of the house.

"What are you doing here?"

"I need to go back to the telegraph office."

"Okay. I'm not stopping you. And I'm not going with you, either." She crossed her arms and leveled him with a look that defied argument.

"Olivia, I know men have a reputation for not knowing what they did wrong half the time, and I thought I was exempt from that rule, but apparently, I'm at the top of the list. I'm not asking you to tell me right now, but we are going to talk about this later. However, right now, there is a situation that needs my attention. It has nothing to do with the bandits, but since I won't be at my place for an hour or so, will you please stay in the house and lock the doors until I return? I need to know you're safe. Please."

Her gaze flickered from his face to the ground, and back again. He was afraid she was going to be stubborn and refuse, but when she gave one brief nod, he let out a breath he didn't realize he'd been holding.

"Thank you. I'll be back as soon as I can." He took a step toward her but stopped when she backed up. Now was not the time to expect her to allow him to show affection. Maybe after they talked about whatever it was that put the bee in her bonnet.

***

James hurried to the telegraph office, anxious to find out more about his dear friend. All the while, he thought about ways he could help. One thing was sure, he needed to go there and personally check on her. He was certain that he was the only person who could convince her to see reason. Although, given recent circumstances, perhaps he wasn't as reasonable as he previously thought. He rolled his eyes at his own plight.

By the time he reached the telegraph office, he had decided to ask Olivia to come with him to Orchard Grove. He was certain his sister Ellie would look after the children until they returned. Persuading Olivia to allow it might prove tricky, but he was not comfortable leaving her here with no one to count on should trouble arise. She simply must come with him. It would also allow them the time they needed to talk about whatever was bothering her.

"*What happened? What about the boarding house? Respond immediately. James*"

James sent his wire to Matt and told the clerk to find him at the sheriff's office when the response came, but before he could turn to leave, another wire came. This one was from Roger. "*Another property found abandoned. Widow fled. Bandits struck again. RJ.*" James clenched his fist and pounded it on the counter before turning to stalk across the street to see Ben.

"Another report of an abandoned property. This one is in a small mining town just beyond Orchard Grove." He pushed out a hard breath. He was glad he wasn't the deputies responsible for finding criminals, but as an officer of the law, he desperately wanted to put these guys away. The longer it went on, the longer they would spend behind bars. He didn't care what their excuses were. Enough was enough.

"Do they have enough help out that way? Do I need to send a few of our men?"

"Matt has several men he trusts. These guys are just slippery, as we well know. They really took a chance coming to our larger town, but with Reicher being part of the gang, they probably figured to put out feelers and see what they could get away with."

"It's good you already knew some of what was going on, so we weren't completely blindsided. Still, I'm sorry they preyed on Missus Martin. She didn't deserve that. None of them do. Do you have any suggestions on how we can help?"

"Well, I got word a little while ago that a dear old lady friend who owns the boarding house in Orchard Grove broke her leg and won't let anyone help." James chuckled. "She's a spirited thing, so it doesn't surprise me much. I need to go there and check on her. I plan to find someone who can run the place for her until she's back on her feet, and I want to bring her back here to recover. She won't like it, but I won't take no for an answer. I'll meet with Matt and maybe we can come up with a plan. I'll wire you if we need you to send reinforcements."

"That sounds like a good plan. What about Missus Martin? Not sure I can get someone to guard her place on such short notice but will do what I can."

James scratched his chest, then glanced out the door. "I plan on taking her with me if she's not too stubborn to agree."

Ben barked a laugh. "Is there trouble in paradise?"

James frowned at him. "No. I don't know."

Ben's wise eyes studied him. "I can see that something happened by the crease on your forehead. I haven't seen that before, but I'm pretty sure it's not just out of concern for your friend with the broken leg."

"Let's just say I'm not sure why I'm in the doghouse, but I intend to find out."

Ben nodded. "Seems like a sound idea. Just let me know if her place needs protection while you're gone. When do you aim to leave?"

They were interrupted by the telegraph operator delivering the response he was waiting for.

"Slipped on wet kitchen floor. Thought to ask Gretchen for help with house. MO."

James grabbed a piece of paper and wrote two messages for the man to send out for him. One going to Matt said, *"Coming today. Hoping to bring help."* The second one was for Roger. *"Will be in OG this afternoon. Contact me there before noon tomorrow with further reports."*

"Please send these for me."

"Yes, sir. Right away."

"Thanks, Timmy." James paid the operator, and the man scurried back to his office to send the wires. Then to Ben, he said, "To answer your question, I'm leaving today, as soon as I can arrange everything. It's just mid-morning, so I should be able to get there before dinner. I can cook a meal for any boarders who are staying. My hope is that until we can get someone local to come take care of things, Olivia will jump in and do what she can while I work on Missus Fields."

"Wire me if you have updates on the bandits. I'll just plan on keeping an eye on Olivia's house whether she goes with you or not."

"I will, and thank you. See you soon."

James started making a mental list of things that needed done before they could leave town. The first thing on his list was his strategy for convincing Olivia to go with him. He was thinking so hard that he nearly stepped out onto the street in front of a wagon.

"James! You just about got yourself killed! What are you doing, stepping out in front of me like that?" his sister Ellie said from her perch. He had to shade his eyes from the sun so he could see her face. After his initial surprise, he realized she was just the person he needed to talk to.

"How else was I supposed to get your attention to slow down so I could talk to you?" he grinned up at her. "Where are you headed in such a rush?"

"I'm not in a rush. It's you who was woolgathering and not paying attention. What are you doing uptown?"

"I'm on a mission. Do you have a few minutes? I wanted to talk to you about something."

"For my favorite big brother? Always!" She smiled, and he climbed up onto the seat beside her. "Where are we headed?"

"Take me to my place while we talk."

She snapped the reins and got the team moving again. She glanced over at him, curiosity playing across her face. "What's on your mind?"

He returned her gaze, pulling his thoughts onto the task at hand. "One of my favorite people from my circuit days has broken her leg. She's an elderly lady who runs a boarding house in Orchard Grove, and I got pretty close to her over the years. She's like a grandmother to me. I need to go see what I can do to help her, but with the trouble that has been going on here for Olivia, I'm worried about leaving her alone. I want to bring her along, partly because I think she can help me convince Missus Fields to come back with me, and partly for selfish reasons." He grinned, and found Ellie smiling, laughter in her eyes.

"Uh-huh. I knew there was something going on that neither of you wanted to admit. I think that's great, James. Really. She's a sweet woman. I think you two would be good for each other."

"Right. So do I. I'm trying to be careful and still give her time to adjust to the idea of a new relationship, but I did let her know that I'll wait as long as it takes. That's not what I wanted to talk to you about though. I need your help convincing her to go with me today. She will argue about needing to be here for the children, which is where I was hoping you would come in."

"Say no more. I can take them. In fact, Naomi has been begging for more time with Frannie, especially since the wedding. That will be easy. And the boys are right around the same age as Michael. Boys don't fuss about needing their friends as much as girls do, but I'm sure they'll get along famously. Let's just go straight to her house and tell her the plan."

James's face turned a bit red. "Well, there might be another roadblock. Earlier today, I must have done or said something wrong, because she seemed to be mad at me. I told her we would talk later, but that was only about an hour ago. I'm not sure she will be willing to spend that much time with me this soon."

Ellie burst out laughing. While she struggled to regain control, she patted his knee. "Make your case for this trip, then skedaddle and let me work my magic."

James had the good grace to look offended, making her laugh again. "But there are details we need to work out. I will need to go to the plantation to borrow a wagon and team. I guess I can ride Justice out there to get them while she gets ready, but it would be easier to do that on the way to Orchard Grove."

"Didn't you use her team and wagon the other day? Why can't you do the same again?"

"I don't want to assume anything. But you're right, let's go there first and talk to her."

Chapter Eighteen

Olivia sat with her hands folded in her lap. It was a pleasant day: warm, but not too warm, with a few fat white clouds floating lazily across the sky. She was trying hard to find a way to talk to James. She felt horrible for how things had gone this morning, but she wasn't sure how to bring it up. He seemed to be his normal cheerful self, and she didn't want to darken the mood. He was right, though. They needed to talk about it.

She had been angry earlier, and had taken it out on him, but she hadn't been sure *why* she was angry. He hadn't really done anything wrong, other than tease her and try to charm his way into her heart. Maybe that's why she felt angry. She knew it would be so easy to let him in and allow him to love her the way he said he wanted to, but she felt guilty for entertaining the idea.

After he asked her to stay locked in the house this morning, she had wanted to rebel and go to the cemetery anyway to talk to Peter, but she was a woman of her word, and once she agreed to stay inside, she stayed. Staying didn't make her angry. In fact, part of her softened toward him for caring.

While she went about her chores, she realized that it had been quite some time since she felt the need to run to Peter's grave. That must mean something. Did it mean her heart was ready to accept love again? She was most definitely attracted to James, and until yesterday at his sister's wedding, she found herself getting angry even contemplating the notion. Since then, however, she discovered that her thoughts leaned toward reciprocating his affection.

Then, when he returned with Ellie and explained that his friend needed their help, she started to refuse, but Ellie proved most efficient, refuting every one of her arguments with a practical solution, leaving Olivia with no reason not to go with him to help his friend. She sighed. *I wonder what James is thinking about. I guess*

I won't know unless I ask him, she giggled to herself. She felt James glance over at her, then he began whistling, and her heart felt a little lighter.

The first hour of their journey had passed in silence except for the sounds coming from the horses. She knew he was giving her time to process her thoughts so that when they did start talking, she would know what she wanted to say. While they had been preparing to leave town, Ellie went back to her house and packed a basket of food for them to eat while they drove. She knew James wanted to reach their destination by late afternoon, so they hadn't taken time to eat before leaving. Surely, he must be getting hungry by now, so perhaps that was a good enough reason to start talking.

Shyly looking at his profile, she tried to find the words. It didn't help much when he looked over at her and smiled. Butterflies took flight in her belly, and she swallowed hard.

"Um, James, are you hungry yet?"

"Actually, I am. How about if I find a spot for a picnic?"

"I assumed you would want to keep moving. If you can eat while you drive, I can hand you a sandwich. I know you want to reach Orchard Grove by late afternoon."

He studied her for a moment. "I appreciate your thoughtfulness. Thank you. That would be wonderful."

She reached down and opened the basket by her feet. Ellie had filled it with sandwiches, fruit, pickles, a jar of nuts, and jars of cold sweetened tea. She handed him a sandwich to start with, waiting to see how he did juggling food and reins before getting one for herself. He seemed to notice that she was waiting and motioned for her to help herself. The next time she glanced at him, he winked.

That man! How was she supposed to have a serious conversation with him when he kept flirting with her? She could feel her cheek flaming, and when she glanced at him again, he had the most self-satisfied grin on his face. She started laughing.

"What's so funny, missy?" James asked around a bite of his sandwich.

"I'm laughing at you. Why were *you* laughing?" she threw the question back at him, which made him laugh harder. She leaned down and retrieved a jar of tea so he could wash down his sandwich before he choked on it. Grinning, she shook her head at his nonsense.

"I'm laughing because you're just so daggone adorable."

"And how is that funny?"

"It just is. You already know how I feel about you. Nothing is going to change that."

She paused before answering. Now was as good a time as any to try and explain why she reacted the way she did this morning.

"Not even unreasonable behavior?"

James looked at her for a long while. Then he gently took her hand. "Not even." He raised her fingers to his lips and placed a sweet kiss on her knuckles while looking into her eyes. Moisture gathered at the corners of them. "Aww, Darlin', it's okay."

"No, it's not. I didn't treat you fairly, and that was wrong of me. I am sorry."

"Nothing to be sorry for. I'm the one who should be sorry. And I am."

"You? You didn't do anything. That's the problem. All you've done is treat me with kindness and respect, and because I felt guilty for enjoying it, I became angry at myself and took it out on you. That's something you will have to get used to, I suppose, if you intend to be around me much. I tend to get angry with myself for falling short of my own standard. It's something I have had to work on for years, but apparently, I'm still working on it. I hope you can forgive me for this morning."

"Sweetheart, you are already forgiven. And I do intend to be around you a whole lot more. A little bit of sass isn't going to drive me away easily. How about if we just count this as our first quarrel and move on, shall we?" He squeezed the hand he still held and then kissed her knuckles again.

Olivia's heart did a flip as she felt her cheeks get pink. But instead of looking away she held his gaze. A lot of emotion was communicated without words in that moment. She felt a weight lift from her shoulders, a weight she knew he would gladly share with her from now on if she allowed him to.

Hadn't she asked God for strength to carry the burden of rearing her children? Is this how He saw fit to answer, by giving her a capable and willing helper in the shape of James? Right then, she whispered a prayer. *Lord, I have fought you for too long. I've asked for your strength to help me over the last several months, but then I tried to push James away. If he is the one you sent to be my helper, I accept. He has been so loving and kind, and being with him makes me feel safe, but I've been afraid and have felt guilty for* wanting to accept him. *I don't want to be wrong by refusing the blessing you've sent into my life. Please help me know for certain that he is your answer to my prayer.*

***

The rest of the afternoon passed pleasantly, and they arrived in Orchard Grove in good time. James wasn't sure where they would find Missus Fields, so they went first to the sheriff's office to see Matt. James helped Olivia down from the wagon, and was reluctant to remove his hands from her waist. More than anything, he wished he could just wrap his arms around her and hold her. Her quick gasp brought him back to the present and he realized he'd been staring at her mouth.

"Sorry," he mumbled as he took a step back. Hearing a deep chuckle, he looked up toward the building to find Matt, arms crossed over his chest, amusement dancing in his eyes, leaning on the doorframe of the jailhouse.

"I see you brought help."

A growl vibrated in his chest as he placed his hand on Olivia's back, guiding her to the boardwalk in front of the jailhouse. At her questioning look, he winked and whispered, "It's okay."

Stepping in front of the other man, James thrust out his hand. "Matt, you scoundrel, good to see you."

"You too, my friend." Matt took the offered hand, and they shook.

"I'd like you to meet a friend of mine, Missus Martin. Olivia, this is Matt O'Connor, sheriff of this town."

"Pleased to make your acquaintance, sheriff."

"Likewise, Missus Martin. Please, come on into my office."

They followed him into the room and took the seats he offered them.

"I take it you just arrived in town."

"Right. I wasn't sure where to find Missus Fields, but I knew you'd know. Tell me, how is she?"

"I'll be honest, James, she's in a lot of pain. She fell this morning. One of her boarders found her and went for the doctor. They managed to get her to the clinic, but he had to sedate her to move her. She's still over there. I don't know what to do about the boarders. It'll soon be time for their evening meal. After I got your wire, I went and fetched Gretchen to do the cleaning and laundry, just so someone was there if anyone had a problem. Didn't want to leave the place unattended."

"That's good. I'm glad you did. Maybe between her and Olivia, they can come up with a meal for all of them." He looked at Olivia, and she nodded, eager to be of service.

"That's a fine idea. I'm sure Gretchen would appreciate it. You remember how shy she is. Almost scared of her own shadow." Then, speaking directly to Olivia, he added, "She was frightened off by them bandits just before James quit the circuit. She was so scared, she came to hide in her brother's house. Been there ever since. Missus Fields was persistent, though, and befriended her. Poor gal didn't know she wanted a friend until she had Missus Fields." Both men laughed at the reference to the spunky lady. "She's a force to be reckoned with, that one. Whoo-ee! Don't want to be caught at the end of her broom. Anyway, Gretchen ventures into town on occasion to visit at the boarding house. It's good for both of them."

"I'd like to go see Missus Fields before we go to the boarding house. I want her to meet Olivia."

"I see. Sure, you go right ahead, then I'll go to the boarding house with you." His grin made Olivia's cheeks tint, and James shook his head and laughed.

"Before we go, have you heard or seen anything of the bandits?"

"No, but I'm as anxious to find them as the rest of you. Has there been any word from anyone else?"

"Yes, just this morning I had a telegram from Roger. They struck again just west of here. This is getting old. How can they stay out of sight so well? Something has to trip them up eventually."

"It's the strangest thing. Never heard anything like it. Roger's due in here next week. Maybe he'll be able to tell me more."

"He knows I'm in town. I told him to report anything to me here. To be honest, these guys are unpredictable. We suspect one of them got himself deputized by lying to the sheriff in Jessup. He was at the meeting we organized to set up guards at Olivia's place. When he learned we were onto them, he reported to his gang, and they all disappeared. Makes me nervous that they'll try something more now they know we're looking for them. That's one of the reasons I asked Olivia to come with me, for her own protection." He put his arm around her shoulders and tugged her protectively against his side. "Besides that, I prefer her company to my own." He smiled and winked at her when she looked up at him.

The sound of Matt clearing his throat brought their attention back to the topic at hand, and they inched their way toward the door.

"Alright, we'll just go over and check in on Missus Fields. Then when you're ready, we'll go down to her place.

Matt stood and walked to the door with them. "There's something I need to check on right quick, but it won't take long. See you in a few minutes then."

Chapter Nineteen

James offered Olivia his arm as they crossed the street to the medical clinic. It wasn't a far walk, but several people had shouted out friendly greetings to James, and he called each one of them by name. Olivia's opinion of him continued to soar. He was such a good man, and it seemed that everywhere he went, people had a high opinion of him. It made her feel proud to be on his arm.

It didn't hurt that he was so handsome, too. After their lunch and the apologies they both made, conversation flowed smoothly, and they grew closer. She learned a lot about what he had done on the circuit, and she shared bits of her life with Peter. However, the thing that made her pulse race was when he looked into her eyes.

His eyes, she couldn't help but notice, were a fascinating mixture of green and brown. From a distance they simply looked hazel, but up close, one eye was more green, rimmed in brown, the other was more brown, rimmed in green. The effect was - captivating. They were kind, gentle, and, when he was amused or teasing, they twinkled with mischief. How had she avoided falling under his spell for so long?

He stood at least a half a head taller than her. His dark hair was neatly trimmed, just touching his collar, and swooped across his forehead, but the inside corner tended to stand up straight right at the part. It was adorable. He kept his beard neatly trimmed, enhancing his professional appearance. Strong arms were attached to a pair of broad shoulders, perfect for making a woman feel safe.

Now that she had decided to open her heart to him, she was noticing all these details she had previously just "seen". She thought back to before Peter began courting her. She had a list of qualities she wanted in a husband, and she didn't agree to his courtship until she was reasonably sure he checked every box. Should she go back to that list now, or were the requirements different because the needs had changed? In many ways, James was similar enough to Peter to attract her, yet different enough to keep her interested.

They entered the clinic and were greeted by an enthusiastic young lady. She jumped up from behind the desk and bounced over to James with a hug. "James! I can't believe you're here! Did you come because of Missus Fields? She will be so happy to see you. I know I am! How have you been?"

James laughed. "Daisy, I want you to meet a friend of mine, Missus Martin. Olivia, this is Daisy, Doc Winters's daughter. I watched her grow from just a wee tot to the young lady she is now. So how do you like helping your Pa?"

"I love it! He has taught me so much, and he lets me help with surgeries. He says I'm a fast learner and will make a good nurse because I have a gentle, calming way with patients. I'm glad I could be here to help with setting Missus Fields's leg, the poor dear."

"I'm glad you were here, too. How is she doing?"

Some of Daisy's exuberance dimmed. "She's hurting more than she admits. She's convinced it was just a matter of setting a cast and she'd be able to get right back to work, but James, it was her femur that broke. When she slipped on the wet floor, she landed with her thigh on the edge of the bucket. I think it's going to take a while to heal."

Just then, Doctor Winters came in the front door. "I see who shows up when my back is turned!" He pounded James on the back with affection, then the two men shook hands, and James introduced him to Olivia. "I guess I don't need to ask why you're here. I hope you're able to talk sense to her. She won't listen to anyone else. You always manage to sweet talk the ladies, though, so I have faith in you." He grinned and winked at Olivia, letting her know he was teasing.

"I don't know about all the ladies, but a handful of them tend to like me." James chuckled. He no longer feared what Olivia might think. She had admitted to him that she admired his relationship with so many people, but she knew that when he was committed to someone, he had eyes for no other. "I'll do what I can to convince her to let others help her. I brought backup just in case, though."

All eyes moved to Olivia, and her neck suddenly felt hot. She smiled and said, "I'm not sure what I can do to convince her, but I know how to cook and clean."

"Those things will go a long way in convincing her to let you help." Doc's response helped to settle Olivia's nerves. "Come on, I'll take you to see her now."

James grabbed Olivia's hand as they walked down the hall behind Doctor Winters. When he opened the door where Missus Fields was resting, she slowly glanced up, a hazy look in her eyes. She appeared so small and helpless lying in the bed, and Olivia immediately felt compassion for the old woman. She had never been able to enjoy having a grandmother, but even before they were introduced, she grabbed onto the connection she knew they would have.

"James, is that really you? Well, forever more. What are you doing all the way over here?"

"I thought it was about time for a visit."

"Why, you were just here a few weeks ago. Did you miss my cooking that much?"

James chuckled. "You know it. You make the best biscuits I've ever had. I've been wasting away on my own cooking recently, so I came to see if you could fatten me up. Imagine my surprise finding you here, though. What happened?"

"Oh, I just slipped on the wet floor. It's nothing." She shifted in the bed, and, although she tried to hide it, they all noticed that she winced in pain. "Who's your lovely friend, James?"

"This is Missus Martin. I've been helping her with a few things, and she agreed to help with something I need to do."

"Come here, honey, and let me get a better look at ya." Olivia smiled as she moved forward, taking the older woman's soft, wrinkled hand gently in hers. "Sit down here on the bed beside me."

"I'm so pleased to finally meet you, Missus Fields. James has told me so much about you."

"Oh, that whippersnapper. Be careful what you believe. He's a rascal, he is." The affection showing on her face belied her words as she looked over Olivia's shoulder to James. "Eats me out of house and home every time he comes to town. You'd think he never got a decent meal anywhere else. Land sakes, I think he stayed longer in this town than any other just for my cookin'."

Everyone laughed, and James attempted to defend himself. "Well, now, in my defense, it is hard to get a decent meal from the back of a horse. Can't properly carry cooking equipment in a saddle bag, and ingredients are hard to locate on the road. I just saved up my appetite for when I knew I was coming here."

"That's alright, sonny. You know I'll feed you anytime. Now, how about you help me up and take me home. It's time to start dinner for the boarders. I need to fry some chicken, and make some mashed potatoes, and bake a chocolate cake. Still need to finish the laundry and clean the guest rooms. Had a couple of people check out today. You two will need rooms tonight, too. Well, don't just stand there, time's a wastin'."

Olivia exchanged a look with James, then he looked to Doctor Winters for his input. Doc shrugged his shoulders and spoke up. "Agnes, we talked before about how serious your injury is. You won't be able to walk on your leg for a few weeks. You need to stay off it so it heals properly."

"Poppycock. No time for that. I have a business to run."

James stepped up and knelt beside her bed, taking her hand in his and speaking gently but firmly. "Listen to me. I know how hard you work, and how important it is to you. Right now, you are going to have to accept the fact that you need someone to help you. So, if you agree to let Olivia and I take over some of your tasks, maybe Doc will agree to let you go home on the condition you stay off your leg and direct us. What do you say?"

At first, she glowered at him, and Olivia was sure she heard a growl. He continued to stare at her, and finally, her forehead relaxed and her eyes watered.

"Oh, my boy, I don't know what to do. I don't want to admit failure, but this darn leg hurts so much I don't think I can make dinner. Who's going to cook? You can't."

"Honey, that's why Olivia's here. She's a wonderful cook, almost as good as you." He shot a wink and a grin at Olivia, eliciting a smile. "You'll be there to tell us what to do, and we'll do it. We just want you to heal as fast as you can, but you have to obey the doctor for that to happen. Everything will be okay, I promise."

Tears leaked out of the corners of her eyes, and she squeezed his hand, bringing it up to her cheek. "I guess if that's what I have to do, that's what I will do, then. I can't believe this happened, but I'm so glad you're here. You're like the son I never had, taking care of me and bossing me around. Now, let's get out of here."

"Why don't you let me go to your place and get things set up to bring you home first. You'll need a comfortable place to sit in the kitchen. You rest while we're gone, and I'll be back to get you in an hour or so, alright?"

She nodded, then reluctantly settled back into her pillows. Olivia adjusted the blanket and offered her a drink before they left the room. Once outside, she found James questioning the doctor about how to care for her.

"It's highly important that she not put her weight, small as she is, on that leg. I'll fit her with some crutches, but with her age, they will be hard for her to use. It's a good thing she's small, James. I know you can lift her with no problem, but I don't know how we'll help her when you leave since I'm sure you can't stay indefinitely."

"I'm planning to take her home with me. Do you think she'll be up for travel in the next day or so?"

Doc's eyebrows snapped up high on his forehead as he regarded James. "It's so good of you to help her like that. I didn't know that's why you came, but I should have guessed. Did Matt wire you about her?"

"He did, and I'm glad. I told her last time I was here that if she ever needed me, I was only a couple hours away. So here I am. As for following up with her injury, you know my brother in-law is the doctor in Jessup. He's a good man and will take good care of her."

"I trust you. And I know Agnes does too, or she wouldn't have agreed to let you cook dinner for her guests." He chuckled and shook his head. "Let's see how she fares through the night and talk about travel in the morning, alright? I'm sure we can make her a bed in your wagon, and if you go slow enough, she should be able to go with you. Getting her to leave her guests unattended will be the hard part. Good luck with that!" He smacked James on the shoulder, laughed, and walked away.

***

James and Olivia were crossing the street back to where their wagon was parked when someone on horseback called out to him.

"Hello, Roger, what are you doing here? I didn't think you'd be back in town until next week. Everything alright?"

"Can we meet with Matt? I'd like to talk to you both."

"Of course. We were just heading there anyway. Roger, this is Olivia Martin. Olivia, Roger is the fine gentleman who gave me my freedom from the circuit." The men laughed at the joke, and they all filed into Matt's office. Matt looked up from the report he was filling out, surprised to see Roger with them.

"James told me you had trouble over in Pine Gulch. Any updates?"

"That's why I'm here early. Someone apparently overheard the bandits talking in the saloon. There were four of them, dressed in long dark coats, fitting the descriptions given by Missus Martin here, Missus Fields, and a few others who have come to us with information. Sounds like they'd had a lot to drink, or else they're getting sloppy, but they were boasting about how many properties they owned now, but they weren't going to stop until they got rid of the old woman who kept the contract and turned them in. That, of course, meant Missus Fields, but I don't know what they are planning. I figured I would just come on over here this afternoon and lend a hand."

"Alright. As much as I hate to pull my men in, I'll gather a few to keep here in town. It's hard to tell what they're up to, but it's time for this to end." Matt got to his feet and paced the small space, his spurs jingling with each step.

James rubbed his chin thoughtfully. "If I didn't know better, I might think Missus Fields's injury was intentional, but she admitted on her own that she slipped on the wet floor."

"What happened? She's injured?"

"Yeah, she fell and broke her femur. Poor gal is in a lot of pain. Doc says she has to stay off it until it heals sufficiently, but you know her, she wants to cook dinner tonight. Surprisingly, she agreed to allow Olivia to cook if she gives the orders." All three men chuckled.

Matt grabbed his hat and put it on, pulling the front down to hide his eyes. "I'm going to send out a couple of boys to round up some of my men, then go tell Gretchen not to allow any new guests at the boarding house tonight, except the three of you, of course. Are you heading there now?" he asked James.

"Yes, I told Missus Fields we would get a place set up for her in the kitchen so she can tell Olivia how to make fried chicken." He grinned at her. "Then, Doc said I can bring her home. Might need one of you to help get her settled."

"I can help. With Gretchen and Missus Martin there, we should be able to get her comfortable."

Roger spoke up. "I'll wander over to the saloon and see what I can learn. Maybe we'll get lucky and find the varmints before they cause any more trouble.

Count on me for dinner, though. I don't enjoy the food at the saloon." He grinned at Olivia.

They all went out onto the boardwalk. Matt saw a couple of boys near the livery and whistled. They turned, and he motioned for them to come to him. After giving them instructions, he climbed up in the back of the wagon and rode with James and Olivia to the boarding house.

When they arrived, Gretchen was sweeping the front porch. Matt jumped down from the wagon before James set the brake, and arrived at her side before James and Olivia were on the ground. James stood in stunned silence, a smirk growing on his face.

"Well, I'll be," he chuckled.

"What is it?" Olivia asked, puzzled by his reaction.

Laughing, James quickly told her that Matt had been a sworn bachelor for as long as he'd known the man, but the last day he was in town, they had both met Gretchen, a shy, frightened widow. "Apparently they are no longer strangers."

James grinned at Olivia as he pulled her to his side, and together they went up the walk toward the house. Introductions were made, and they all went inside. They all worked together to arrange comfortable seating for their dear friend. Each of them had suggestions, and by the time everything was settled, the ladies were comfortable working together.

Gretchen told them what she had been able to accomplish during the day. She had finished the laundry, swept and mopped the downstairs floors, and cleaned the empty guest rooms. She admitted that she was getting nervous about cooking dinner for so many people and was glad Olivia had arrived to do that.

James broached the topic which had all of them concerned. "Gretchen, I fully intend to take Missus Fields back to Jessup with us and I was wondering if you would feel comfortable taking charge of the boarding house while she's away? I'm not sure how long it will be. It will depend on how well she recovers. At her age, it might not go as well as she hopes. What do you say? Will you do it?"

"Well, I suppose I could. I'm not the best cook, and I'm not used to cooking for a lot of people, but if it will put her mind at ease, I'll do anything."

Matt reached over and squeezed her hand. "You're a good friend, Gretchen. Thank you."

"Yes, thank you. I'm sure that will make it easier to convince her to come with us."

Olivia spoke up then. "She said it was time to start cooking dinner for the guests. Gretchen, do you know how many guests are still registered here? She said some left today. Also, do any of you know where she keeps her supplies? If not, I'm sure we will find things as we go."

James led Olivia to the pantry and helped her gather the ingredients she thought they'd need to make a good dinner, then he and Matt left to go back to the clinic. Olivia started mixing up a chocolate cake while Gretchen peeled potatoes and they soon fell into a comfortable routine, chatting while they worked.

Neither of them noticed the shadowy figures lurking behind the house.

Chapter Twenty

"Now, young man, you put me down!" James ignored the instructions being shouted at him as he carried Missus Fields to the wagon. Before arriving at the clinic, they had stopped at the livery and added a soft bed of straw to the back and covered it with blankets James had brought from home.

"I will just as soon as we get to the wagon." It was more difficult than he expected to carry her without jostling her leg, especially since the injured part was her thigh. He might have to build a chair on wheels so she could get around without continually putting pressure on the break.

Matt was in the wagon, ready to take her from James. Carefully, they got her situated, and once she was settled, Matt hopped into the driver's seat while James sat with her in the back. She barked more orders at them when they arrived at her house, and they grinned at each other.

The smell of chocolate cake baking greeted them when Olivia opened the door to let them in. Rather than making a fuss over the invalid, they welcomed her home. Gretchen had finished peeling potatoes, and was on the back stoop plucking the chickens they would soon be frying for dinner. Missus Fields looked around her sparkling kitchen with grudging approval.

When dinner was ready and everyone was assembled, James pulled Missus Fields's chair closer to the dining table and Olivia set up a tray in front of her for her plate. There were four men in addition to Matt, Gretchen, Roger, James, and Olivia. The guests were sympathetic to Missus Fields's injury and offered to help in any way they could.

Murmurs of appreciation for the flavorful food floated around the table, and Olivia smiled encouragement at Gretchen. The younger woman shyly accepted the implied compliment. Everyone took turns sharing stories of their adventures, and some had all of them laughing.

James, as always, was careful not to tell anything too personal when guests were around, so he shared funny stories about staying at Missus Field's Boardinghouse. The lady laughed until tears rolled down her weathered cheeks, and he was happy to have helped her forget her pain for a little while.

After dinner, the guests each thanked the ladies for the wonderful meal and went their separate ways. James and Matt washed the dishes, insisting the ladies take a break and sit with Roger and Missus Fields. Of course, they refused, but instead went upstairs to check on the guest rooms that Roger, James and Gretchen would be occupying that night. Olivia insisted on sleeping downstairs near Missus Fields in case she needed anything during the night.

When the work was finished, the five of them gathered around the lady of the house. Quiet fell as they anticipated the hard conversation to come. At first, she seemed oblivious to the mood and continued talking to

Roger, explaining her method of planting the garden for the best crop yield. James and Matt seemed to read one another's thoughts, while Olivia and Gretchen talked quietly off to one side.

Finally, Missus Fields seemed to understand that something was amiss. "Alright, boys, what's going on?"

Matt nodded to James, who took a deep breath and began, speaking in low tones so that any guest passing the doorway would not hear. "We have reason to think you are in danger." With her sharp gasp, he gently took her hand, soothing her. "Remember that contract the man in the long dark coat left here?" She nodded. "There is a gang of them. We have been referring to them as the property bandits. We are not sure what their motive is, but they have been driving people out of their homes. It seems each victim is a widow. Gretchen is a victim. Olivia has been approached also. We have had deputies everywhere looking for them for months."

"What does this have to do with me?"

Roger told what he heard. "We think they are targeting you now because you kept the contract they wanted you to sign."

"Right. I took your contract for Matt to see, and we both went to Gretchen to get her story. Around the time I moved back to Jessup, Olivia was approached. First by a man in the cemetery, then by one at her front door. She immediately came to me for help, and since her story was similar to yours and Gretchen's, I went to the sheriff there. We assembled all the deputies and set up around-the-clock guards at her house, but it seems that one of the so-called deputies was also one of the gang. They never returned to demand a signature on their document like they had always done before, and when Ben paid a call to the man we suspect, there was no trace of him or anyone."

Missus Fields's hands were visibly shaking, and Gretchen's face had blanched as he told the story. "Where are they now?"

"We suspect they are heading here. Roger overheard some men over at Pine Gulch. It sounded like they were planning something, but we don't know what. We have men standing by to keep watch overnight, and we're going to take care of you, don't you worry, alright?" Matt crouched in front of her, hand on her arm. He reached into his pocket, pulled out a clean handkerchief, and handed it to her. She took it gratefully and wiped the tears from her eyes.

Olivia spoke. "I'm so sorry this is happening to you, especially right now when you're already hurting from your accident today. All of us will be here to help keep watch. Your biggest job is to rest and heal and let us do the hard stuff." James sent Olivia an appreciative look for her kind words. "Right now, I think we should get you settled in your room so you can get some sleep. This day has been pretty overwhelming for you. James and Matt will get you into your room, and I'll get you something for pain, then we'll leave you alone for a while. I will be sleeping on the dining room couch near your room in case you need someone. I put a spoon and tin cup by your bed. Use it as a bell to alert someone anytime you need something, alright?"

The old woman cast grateful eyes on Olivia. "Thank you, my dear. You have all been so kind to me. I can't tell you how much I appreciate each of you. You are my family. I love you so." Her tears flowed freely now, and she used whatever dry parts she could find on Matt's handkerchief to catch them.

"We all love you, too. That's why we're here to help. Are you ready for us to help you to bed now?"

"Yes, but do you really need to carry me?"

"Unless you think you can fly." James's cheeky remark produced the desired effect, and she smiled.

"Oh, alright. Let's go. I am pretty tired tonight."

***

As the sun set on the western horizon, the town quieted. Matt and Gretchen had gone to his office to see if he had any new messages, and Roger went back to the saloon to see if he could pick up any more information. They hoped someone's tongue would loosen and the gang would get caught before they could do Missus Fields any more harm.

James invited Olivia to go for a walk with him, and they stepped out onto the front porch. It was a beautiful evening with the promise of a moonlit sky. A gentle breeze made the leaves flutter, and birds were settling into their nests for the night.

"I don't want to go far in case she needs me." Olivia hesitated to step off the porch even though James seemed to have no reservations about it.

"We won't go far. I just want to show you something. Come on," he urged gently. Finally, Olivia agreed, and he took her hand in his as they walked slowly to the boardwalk that ran along the edge of the street. Turning away from the central part of town, they walked in the direction of the outskirts, but before they left the boarding house property, he turned them back into the yard. In the distance, Olivia could see a large garden plot. The soil had been turned recently, and rows of vegetables were growing. Everything looked green and healthy.

"What a beautiful garden she has. I hope Gretchen will be able to take care of it for her while she's with us. It would be a shame for her to not have the produce necessary to keep feeding her guests through the winter."

"I know. Part of why I came back here was to see how much she has planted and what might still need to go in. Gretchen comes from a farm, though, so I have no doubt that she can handle this. Come on back here." He took her past the garden to a slope that led to a wide creek. A pretty little bridge had been built over the creek, and the path ended at an orchard of fruit trees. Blossoms covered the branches, promising the potential for a good harvest. At the edge of the orchard was a bench carved from a fallen tree, so they sat down.

"This is such a lovely spot. Thank you for bringing me here."

James remained quiet, his arm draped across the bench behind her, and Olivia suddenly realized he was watching her. A shiver of delight raced up her spine.

"I could do this every day," he whispered.

Stunned, she turned to face him. What did he mean, exactly? If he meant what she thought he meant, was she ready for that? Shouldn't she find out what her children thought about having him as part of their family? Who was she kidding - Frannie and Michael adored him. That would be no problem at all. She shivered again.

"I think you need an Armstrong heater."

"A what?" She was so confused. Peter had been knowledgeable about all the most modern gadgets available to put in the buildings he constructed. He had taught her a lot about his business, but she had never heard of such a thing. "I've never heard of anything like that before. What is it?"

James smiled and got on his feet, pulling her up with him. "This." And he wrapped his arms around her and held her close. Slowly, her arms circled his middle, and she allowed her cheek to rest against his pounding heart. Then, he leaned back slightly, looking deeply into her eyes. When his gaze dropped to her lips, her traitorous tongue darted out to moisten them, and her hand on his chest detected an increase in his heart's rhythm as his lips claimed hers in a sweet and gentle, but possessive kiss.

Olivia thought her knees had turned to jelly. It's a good thing James was still holding her, or she would certainly be on the ground. Oh my! The man could kiss! Suddenly, she decided she wouldn't object to those lips kissing her more often.

James ended the kiss with a shaky breath. He brought his hands up to the sides of her face and pressed his forehead against hers. "Olivia, you drive me crazy."

A nervous giggle escaped her. "I'm sorry."

"No! Don't be. I mean that in a good way." He chuckled and kissed her forehead. "You make me feel like a youngster again, experiencing love for the first time."

"I didn't think it was possible, but you kind of turned my knees to jelly."

James laughed and drew her back into his arms. "Good. I haven't lost my touch. But just to be sure, I'm going to kiss you again." This time, he turned up the heat and made the kiss more passionate. Just when she thought her bones had melted into a puddle, he stepped away from her. "We had better return to civilization before I destroy your reputation."

They walked hand in hand back the way they came, across the bridge, through the yard and onto the boardwalk. By that time, stiffness had returned to her bones, and she felt like she could speak without losing her breath.

"So that's an Armstrong heater, huh?" He heard the amusement in her voice and grinned.

"Yep. Just let me know anytime you want me to show you how it works." He winked at her, and she felt her cheeks grow red. "Would you like something cold to drink? I'll go see what's available if you want to sit out here for a while."

"That sounds nice. Thank you."

James took a moment to check on Missus Fields while he was near the kitchen. Her room was down a short hall behind the dining room. A door leading to the back stoop stood between her room and the kitchen. He checked to make sure it was locked before going back to the kitchen. He was grateful that Olivia had insisted someone sleep close to her, but he wished she would let him be the one. He wanted her to have a decent bed instead of the couch in the dining room.

The woman was amazing. He was so glad she agreed to accompany him on this trip. He knew he could count on her to do whatever was necessary to see that things were taken care of for the guests. She had put Missus Fields at ease and, with Gretchen's help, had cooked a wonderful meal of which even the older woman approved.

He didn't know much about Gretchen before tonight, but she seemed to be dependable, also. Maybe Matt was seeing himself settling down with her. James grinned. He could see them being happy together. After what Gretchen had been through, from losing her husband then losing her home to the bandits, she deserved someone stable like Matt.

James heard voices on the porch. It sounded like Matt and Gretchen had returned. He grabbed two extra glasses and the pitcher of sweetened tea and went out to join the others. After pouring drinks for everyone and passing them around, he and Matt walked over to the far side of the porch for a private conversation.

"James, do you have your sidearm with you?"

"Of course. I always carry it, especially when I travel."

"Good. Don't be afraid to use it if necessary."

"Is there more news?"

"I didn't want to alarm the ladies, but as we were walking back over here, I saw some men go into the saloon. It was getting dark, but they appeared to match the description of our guys. I'm going over there soon to see what they're up to, then I'll be taking the first watch. I have a few other men scheduled throughout the night. I just wish I knew what to expect."

"Count on me to take my turn, Matt. I want them caught as bad as you do."

"I know you do. I'd like to be a fly on the wall in that saloon. Surely they'll say something to clue us in. Hopefully Roger will hear something."

They discussed the plan for keeping watch, then rejoined the women for more conversation. To James's amusement, Olivia was asking Gretchen about preserving vegetables and fruits. They finished their drinks, then Olivia hid a yawn and declared it was time to get some sleep. She took the pitcher and Gretchen gathered glasses, then they said goodnight to James and Matt and went inside.

A gunshot sounded from the direction of the saloon. Matt, instantly alert, took off at a run with James on his heels.

Chapter Twenty-One

Four figures rushed past James and Matt, almost knocking them down in their haste. In the darkness, it was impossible to identify them, but James turned to watch them briefly. However, both men were in a hurry to see what had happened inside the saloon. Knowing that Roger was inside made them concerned for his well-being.

As they entered, the owner of the establishment looked up from the man on the floor. "Sheriff, thank God you're here. This man was shot, and the man who shot him just ran out the door with his friends." Matt and James made eye contact, but rather than go after them, they turned their attention to the victim.

A groan sounded from the man on the floor. James bent down to see what he could do to help, but the injured man was lying face down in a pool of blood and a towel had been pressed to the wound on his back. He glanced up at Matt, and they worked together to carefully roll the victim onto his back. When they turned him over, their fear was confirmed: it was Roger.

As gently as possible, a few men helped James carry an unconscious Roger down the street to the clinic where Doctor Winters met them and held open the door.

"Take him to the first room on the left, gentlemen. Lay him on the table while I make sure I have the supplies I need. I heard the shot and figured someone would be along shortly. Anyone know this man?"

James spoke up, voice low and solemn. "Yes, his name is Judge Roger Jefferies. He's the man who replaced me on the circuit." The men who had helped carry him glanced at one another, eyes wide. Doc just nodded.

James watched Doc work, offering his help, while the other two went back to the saloon. "Any idea who did this?" Doc asked as he cut away Roger's shirt and doused the wound with carbolic acid to help stave off infection. It appeared that the bullet had gone all the way through, having entered from the front of his shoulder. Fortunately, nothing vital had been hit, but he would need to check the damage done to vessels since he had already lost a lot of blood.

"Not yet. Matt and I were sitting on the porch of the boarding house, discussing a problem some folks are facing all over the region when we heard the gunshot. It sounded like it came from this direction, so we ran over here right away. As we approached the saloon, four men rushed past us, so I suspect they had something to do with it, but I don't know who they were. Neither of us recognized them, but Matt is over there questioning people now."

Doctor Winters glanced up at James, then continued working on stitching up the wound on the back of Roger's shoulder. "I hope Matt finds them. If Roger here is anything like you, he didn't do anything to provoke them. But, you know, people get shot for a lot of reasons. Could be, the shooter just didn't like where Roger was sitting, or how he looked. Maybe his dog died, and he was just mad at the world. Could be any number of things. Glad it's not my job to figure it out. It's just my job to patch up the unlucky ones."

"Yeah, and it was my job to decide just how guilty the guilty party was, and to determine how long they should be kept locked up. Whether the victim lives or dies plays a big role in the sentencing. It wears on a man." James muttered the words, as though thinking out loud, then shook his head sadly over the depraved nature of mankind.

Doc sighed deeply. "As long as we can get the bleeding stopped, and as long as he doesn't get an infection, this guy has a pretty good chance of living through it. He'll be sore for a good, long time, though. There's damage to the muscle tissue, and of course, nerves will be affected. Only time will tell how well he regains strength in that arm, but we'll know more come morning. Here, help me turn him over now so I can work on the hole on the front side."

While they rolled Roger, James thought about what the doctor had said. *He didn't do anything to provoke them*. Oh, no! Four men, running from the saloon. Roger shot senselessly. They had to have been the bandits! How had he not seen it before? They must have somehow recognized Roger and figured out he was watching for them. That meant Missus Fields might be in danger, and possibly Olivia, too! He needed to get back to the saloon and talk to Matt right away!

"Doc, I need to go! I think Missus Fields is in trouble! Will you be okay here by yourself?"

"Yes, yes, you go! Daisy is upstairs if I need her. Go!"

Without another word, James ran from the clinic back to where he had last seen Matt. As he approached the saloon, he saw four horses with riders leaving the livery and heading out of town at a gallop. He rushed into the saloon, yelling for Matt.

"Matt! Bandits, riding out of town in a hurry!"

Matt spun around and ran out the door. Several men ran with him, and they all headed to the livery where Matt's horse always stood ready. James was torn, wanting to assist in taking down the bandits, but instead, he rushed back toward the boarding house.

Before he was halfway there, he heard shouts of "Fire! Fire at the boarding house!" His heart plummeted even as he increased his pace, his first thought being for Olivia. By the time he arrived, the church bell was ringing, calling for volunteers to come help with the emergency in town.

James raced down the street, arriving just in time to hear the windows breaking in the kitchen and see flames licking up the outside walls on that end of the house. Panicked, he yelled for Olivia. He kept calling for her as he burst through the front door. Heat and smoke forced him to slow his steps, but he continued calling to her. "Lord, please help me find her. Keep her safe!"

Yanking a curtain from the parlor window, he covered his head and shoulders and went toward the back of the house where he knew Missus Fields was sleeping. He had to get her out of here! She would be unable to get out under her own power. He kept calling. "Olivia? Gretchen? Someone, please answer me!"

He made his way through the smoke to the back of the dining room and found that the couch was empty except for a few linens and pillows. Good! Olivia wasn't there. But where was she? Pushing his way to the back hall, he noticed the door to the outside standing open. After calling out again, he heard his name coming between coughs from a voice in the distance.

"James!" cough, cough, "we're out here!"

Running out the back door, away from the burning kitchen, he went straight to the cluster of huddled people near the creek. He gathered Olivia in his arms for a quick hug, then looked into her eyes.

"Are you okay? Are you hurt? Burned?"

"No, I'm fine. I just inhaled a little bit of smoke. Thank the Lord we're all okay."

Suddenly realizing he was focused only on Olivia, James then looked around to see who else was there. Gretchen was sitting on a blanket on the ground, bracing up a stunned Missus Fields.

"What about Gretchen and Missus Fields? Are they okay? Where are the men who are staying here? Were they even here?"

"Yes, they're over there helping put out the fire. And Gretchen and Missus Fields are shaken, but unharmed.

Pulling her to him again, he kissed her temple. "Ah, Sweetheart, I was so frightened when I heard someone yelling that there was a fire here. I had to make sure you were safe. All of you." He let out a shaky breath, the traumatic events of the night finally catching up with him. "I suppose I should go help put out the fire now that I know you are okay."

"James, look up there."

He looked toward the house and found an efficient group of townspeople working together to put out the fire. They had a water wagon and hoses. Men took turns pumping while others formed a bucket line. Even younger boys were helping by retrieving buckets full of water from the creek and running them back to the line. He was impressed with how well everyone worked together to try and save the house.

Tightening the arms that were still around Olivia, he said, "This town has some really great people. But are you sure you're all okay? Do you need anything?"

"We'll be fine. We have several blankets, so we can sit on those and wrap some around us." The emotional trauma had her shivering, and James bent to grab a blanket to wrap around her shoulders.

"Before I go see if I can help, do you have any idea how this happened?"

"No. I was just dozing off when I heard glass break, then smoke was filling the kitchen and flames were everywhere."

"You did a wonderful job of getting everyone out without injury. I'm so proud of you." He kissed her forehead and rubbed her arms affectionately.

She smiled. "After I realized there was smoke and fire in the house, I yelled for everyone upstairs. I even banged on the tin mug with the spoon I had given Missus Fields, hoping the additional noise would rouse them. Fortunately, most of them were not solidly asleep yet. I was afraid to leave Missus Fields, but was also afraid they wouldn't hear me. One of the men must have heard me first, and he started shouting for the others. A couple of the men carried Missus Fields out here while Gretchen and the others gathered the blankets." Tears began to slide down her cheeks, making sooty trails. "James, I was so worried because I didn't know where you and Matt were. Last I knew you were on the front porch, but I was afraid you might be upstairs sleeping."

"Ah, Honey, I'm sorry. No, we *were* on the porch. Until we heard a gunshot."

She gasped and covered her mouth. "Oh, dear! Where was that?"

"At the saloon. Matt and I ran over there and found that Roger had been shot."

"Oh no!! Is he - is he - will he be okay?" Her voice quivered.

He put his arms around her. "He should be fine. Some men helped me carry him to the clinic while Matt questioned people. I helped hold him still while Doc sewed him up, but something Doc said made me start to think. We were talking about why someone would shoot him, and he said, 'If he's anything like you, he didn't do anything to provoke them.' That's when I realized we had been almost knocked down by four men running from the saloon. Most likely the four men we've been looking for all this time. As you know, we were concerned they were after Missus Fields, so I'm surprised - and aggravated - it took me so long to make the connection, and now I'm curious why Matt didn't go after them immediately. I ran back to the saloon to tell Matt my suspicions, but on my way there, I saw four horses, with riders, speeding out of town. Matt and his guys took off after them while I came to check on you all. That's when I heard about the fire. I'm just so relieved you all got out." He held her close again and kissed her hair. "Are you sure you're not hurt?"

"I'm fine. I checked with everyone else, and they are all unharmed. Stunned, but okay. Once we got a safe distance away, they all rushed back to help. Missus

Fields has just been staring, unblinking, since we got out here, though. I'm very concerned about her, James."

James scratched his cheek, then said, "Let me check on everyone at the house and let them know I can come back later, then I'll go get the wagon so we can take her back to the clinic and have Doc check her over. She's probably in shock. The poor thing has been through a lot of horrible things today. The pain medication you gave her would make her groggy, and having been awakened so abruptly might be a contributing factor, also. I'll be back as soon as I can. Stay right here." He hugged her again, kissed her forehead, then was gone.

Chapter Twenty-Two

The golden fingers of early dawn were beginning to chase away the night by the time Matt and his deputies rode back into town. It had been a long night, chasing shadowy figures across the county. As Matt suspected, they had headed toward Jessup, presumably intent on destroying Olivia's home, but Ben was watching over her place and intercepted the bandits.

The strong smell of smoke was still in the air, and Matt's concern overrode his exhaustion. As he and the others swung off their mounts at the livery, Andrew, the stable master, greeted them, covered with soot and a weariness that was uncharacteristic of the young man.

"Was there a fire here last night, Andrew?"

"Sheriff, it was plumb awful. The boarding house burnt. The whole town helped put out the fire though."

Matt's face went ashen. Gretchen was staying there, as well as Olivia, and a few guests, and of course Missus Fields. Good lord! What happened?

"Did everyone get out of there?"

"Oh yeah, Missus Martin called out and woke up all the guests, and they got Missus Fields out. James took her to the clinic to make sure she weren't hurt."

"Where's everyone now? Surely they couldn't stay there last night."

"All I know is James is over at the jailhouse."

"Thanks, Andrew."

"Say, Sheriff, did ya catch them fellers you took off outta here after?"

"Sure did!" Matt said with a grin. He tipped his hat toward Andrew as he left the livery and headed to the jailhouse.

Matt entered his office, expecting to find James asleep in one of the cells. Instead, Missus Fields' guests were occupying the cots, and James was making a pot of coffee.

"Mornin'. Imagine finding you here." Matt's grin was tired, but he was glad to see his friend.

"Well, we had a little problem around here last night."

"Yeah, I heard. Andrew told me about it. Said everyone is safe. Where are Gretchen and Olivia?"

"They're over at the clinic. Doc gave Missus Fields a bed, and Daisy insisted on the ladies staying there with the family."

"And they're alright? Not burned or anything?"

"By the grace of God, no. Olivia heard glass break, then smoke and flames started filling the kitchen. She roused everyone from upstairs, and some of the men carried Missus Fields outside to the creek. All the guests helped with the fire. As you were taking off out of town, I ran back toward the boarding house. I heard people shouting about the fire and I have to tell you, Matt, I was terrified I would lose Olivia, right when we just found each other. Finding her was all I could think about as I burst through the front door, and when she didn't answer right away, well, let's just say it was a pretty scary moment. Such relief swept over me when I heard her calling my name from outside!"

"I can imagine. I knew there was something between you two. I'm happy for you, James, real happy." Matt grinned as he felt some of that relief sweep over him, as well.

"Thanks, man. After I checked on them, I went to help with the fire, but there were so many townspeople working on it, I decided that with what Missus Fields had already been through yesterday, it was more important to get her under Doc's care."

"I agree. That was a good idea. Say, how's Roger? I know you stayed with him for a while when I was questioning people in the saloon. What happened? And how did you know the riders were leaving town?"

"The bullet went through his shoulder. He lost a lot of blood, but no serious damage other than holes that need to heal, and for nerves and muscles to return to normal. Of course, the next day or two will determine if he gets an infection from it."

"I'm relieved to hear that. We'll just pray he recovers fully."

James nodded in agreement. "Doc was asking me about who he was, and said if Roger was anything like me, he wouldn't have provoked those guys into shooting him. After he said that, I suddenly remembered getting almost knocked over by four men leaving the saloon after we heard the gunshot, and I realized Missus Fields was probably in trouble. My guess is the ones you chased are the ones who shot Roger."

Matt paced around the small office, coffee mug in hand. "Yep, and the ones who set the fire to destroy the boarding house."

"Daggone. Now it's making more sense. Did you catch up with them?"

"Oh yeah! We got 'em. Chased 'em all the way to Jessup!"

James's jaw dropped, realization dawning. "They were headed to Olivia's place next."

"Yep. Sheriff Richardson happened to be patrolling the area and heard them coming. He got out of sight and watched, but by then we were on their tail. They musta been feeling the squeeze, because they dismounted and got ready to shoot at us. Ben waited until we got closer, then took their attention away from us. We were able to arrest all four without further incident."

"That's great! So, where are they now?"

"He kept them there since your jailhouse is bigger than mine. He identified one of them as Aerick Reicher and singled him out. Put some pressure on him to identify the others and admitted they were the ones doing the illegal swindling of widows out of their homes. Also confirmed it was only four of them. I'll be back up there to add my questions, especially since a shooting and arson will be added to their charges."

"Good. I'm glad that's over." James looked out the window and grinned. "We're about to get some company." He went to the door and opened it for Olivia and Gretchen.

"Good morning, James. We brought you and the guests some food. Matt! You're back!"

James glanced at Gretchen just in time to see her eyes grow wide and a soft pink color creep up her neck to her cheeks. Smiling, he looked over at Matt, who couldn't look away from Gretchen. He chuckled and met Olivia's eyes. Apparently, she had noticed the same thing, and they both grinned.

Clearing his throat, James asked, "How are our patients today?"

"Missus Fields slept most of the night. She's had breakfast and more medication for her pain and is sleeping again. Daisy stayed with Roger through the night, and he woke up just a little bit ago. He has some pain, but she said it's good news that he's awake and doesn't have any sign of fever yet. They'll keep him there for a couple of days, especially since there's no boarding house to go to, and he needs time to recover."

After they cleaned up from breakfast, they all went to the boarding house to see what kind of damage there was. Smoke had permeated the entire structure, but the worst of the fire damage was in the kitchen, the walls surrounding it, and the dining room.

For James, it was confirmation that Missus Fields needed to go back to Jessup with him and Olivia. Gretchen volunteered to do the cleaning necessary to make the bedrooms inhabitable again and Matt offered to help as much as he could, but until the kitchen could be rebuilt, the boarding house would have to be closed. All the guests gathered their personal belongings and went to find other lodging.

Matt inspected the kitchen, trying to locate the source of the fire. He found broken glass from a whisky bottle, further confirmation that the fire had been intentionally started. Not that they needed it. He figured Ben could pull an admission of guilt from Reicher if necessary.

When they were finished at the boarding house, they all went to the clinic to see Missus Fields and Roger. As they arrived at the door to Missus Fields's room, they heard the doctor talking with her.

"I'm sure James will be here soon. He brought you here because he was concerned about you."

"I just don't know why he took me out of my bed in the middle of the night to bring me here. I wanted to sleep in my own bed. This one is hard and uncomfortable. I hardly slept a wink all night."

"Did I hear my name?" Olivia smiled at how smoothly James inserted himself in the conversation.

"Young man, I want you to take me home now. There's no need to be fussin' over me. I got work to do. Help me up."

"Now, did you forget about your broken leg? You're not going to be cooking and cleaning for anyone for a while." James glanced at Olivia and winked.

"Hogwash. It's got to get done somehow, and I'm the one who's got to do it. Now, get me up." She struggled onto her elbows and Olivia rushed forward to stack a few more pillows behind her. "You're a good girl, Olivia. A right good girl."

Olivia blushed, and James beamed. Then, Missus Fields realized Matt and Gretchen were also outside her room.

"What are you two doing out there? Everyone else is here, you may as well come in, too," she hollered. "Matt, if James won't take me home and let me do my work, you will, won't you." She said it more as a statement than a question.

"Well, now, ma'am, there's some things we need to talk about."

"Such as?"

"See, there was a fire last night. Do you remember it at all?"

"A fire? That's awful! Where?"

Matt knelt by her bed and took her hand in his. "At the boarding house."

Her cheeks went pale. "What happened?"

"Well, remember the men who wanted you to sign those papers?" She nodded slowly, watching him warily. "See, there's a gang of 'em, and when they found out we knew about 'em, they came back to try to hurt you. They set your house on fire. I'm sorry to say, it's a big mess. Gonna take a while to get it fixed up again."

Tears started rolling down the old lady's cheeks. Olivia handed her a handkerchief and wrapped her arm around her shoulders, holding her close.

"What-t am I g-gonna d-d-do? It's all I have left of my G-Gus" She began to sob. James went to the other side of her bed and sat on the edge, pulling her toward his chest. They sat there for several minutes until she gained some control.

Matt spoke up. "Gretchen and I will work on getting the smoke cleaned out of the house, but it will take some time. No one will be safe sleeping there for a while. Unfortunately, the kitchen is destroyed. I'm so sorry."

"B-but I don't have anywhere else to stay. Can you just fix up my room so I can stay there?"

James held her away from him and looked into her eyes. "Remember how I made you promise me that if you ever needed anything to let me know?" She squinted at him. "This is that time. You are going to come home with me, and Olivia, my mama and sisters and I will all take care of you while your leg mends."

More tears poured down her cheeks.

"Olivia was here with you throughout the night, and she has proven to be an excellent nurse. You'll be in good hands with her, Agnes. I'll make sure she has all the instructions and medication you'll need. Besides, I hear James has a brother-in-law who is almost as good a doctor as I am." Doctor Winters smiled at her, then said, "I'll let you all continue making your plans, but I see no reason why you can't leave this afternoon. Meanwhile, I have another patient to check on."

They stayed with the elderly lady for a while longer, reassuring her and including her in the plans they were making for the trip that afternoon, then left her to rest while they went to check on Roger. He was sleeping, so their questions about the incident that happened in the saloon would have to wait until later. After asking Daisy to come get him when Roger was alert, Matt returned to his office, taking Gretchen with him.

James and Olivia went back to the orchard behind the boarding house. So much had happened since the last time they were there such a short time ago, but they both felt the need to be alone together. James opened his arms, and she willingly went to him. He held her close, and she clung to him, then he lifted her chin until she was looking into his eyes.

"Olivia, I know a lot has happened since yesterday morning, but one thing is very clear to me. I feel like I've waited most of my life for you, and that's been a long time." She smiled. "I don't want to wait any more. I know that I love you and I want to spend the rest of my life with you. Will you marry me?"

Tears gathered in the corners of her eyes as she gazed into his. First one, then another ran over and fell down her cheeks.

"Honey, I'm sorry. If it's too soon, I can wait." His thumbs gently wiped away her tears, then he whispered, "You're worth waiting for."

She put her fingers over his lips and smiled through her tears. "I have learned a lot recently. For the longest time, I didn't feel worthy of love. Not from God. Not from you. But I've reconciled that with God, and I've discovered that I can love and be loved. I no longer need to feel guilty or angry, or even unworthy. I just need to let love in." She paused, studying his face. "But," James stopped breathing, and his pulse raced. "Before I give you my answer, I think we need to seek the approval of two others who will be directly affected by my decision. We have to ask Frannie and Michael."

He pressed a sweet kiss to her brow. "You're right, of course. Let's go home!"

Smiling and laughing, they walked back to town, hand in hand.

Chapter Twenty-Three

"Mama! You're here! And Mister MacKay! Frannie! They're here!" Michael jumped from the porch of the plantation house and ran to the wagon to meet them, Toby running alongside him, wagging his big, bushy tail and barking a happy greeting. Frannie and Naomi came meandering from the barn, each of them snuggling as many kittens as they could hold. James chuckled at the scene, and Olivia laughed as she waited for James to help her down from the wagon.

As James lowered her to the ground, hands around her waist, their eyes met, and he almost forgot they had an audience. With a smirk, he quickly stepped away and winked at her, grinning when she blushed. She shook her head at him, and he chuckled, then went to the back of the wagon to help Missus Fields.

They had waited until after an early lunch to leave Orchard Grove. Doc had insisted that Missus Fields have another dose of laudanum so that she could better endure the trip. James had asked Andrew at the livery to add extra layers of straw to make the ride more comfortable for her, and Olivia and Gretchen packed snacks that they had purchased at the mercantile and prepared in the Winters's kitchen.

Just before lunch, Roger had been awake and alert enough for James and Matt to interview him about the shooting. James thought back over the conversation while he watched Olivia greet her children.

"Do you remember what happened last night?" Matt asked.

"I was just minding my own business, sipping a cold beer, listening to conversation around me and watching four men who didn't seem to fit in. I overheard them talking about 'bringing an end to this', and my ears perked up. Mostly, they were pretty quiet, and I couldn't hear much, just a snippet now and then. But those words made the hair on the back of my neck

stand up. I guess I made eye contact with one of them, because he got really angry and aggressive, stood up, knocking the table into his friends. Then, of course, they were all on their feet, coming at me. I'm not sure how much they'd had to drink, but they were definitely not sober. I raised my hands in surrender, like an apology, but the hotheaded one pulled his gun and the next thing I knew, I was on the floor with a hole in my shoulder."

"Can you describe them? You said there were four. Did they associate with any other patrons or keep to themselves?"

Roger stroked his chin with his right hand. "Yep, four of them. They pretty much kept to themselves, talking like they were reviewing some plans they had. One was tall and blond, a nice looking fella. One was small with dark hair and shifty eyes, like he was afraid of his own shadow. The other two were average height and build, brown hair, but the mean one had a scar on his forehead. All of them were clean shaven and wore those long, dark dusters. I'm guessing they were the men we've been wanting to find?"

Matt grinned. "Yep. And we got 'em. They're cooling off in jail over in Jessup as we speak."

Roger smiled. "Good! Then my souvenir here was worth getting." He indicated the bandage over the wound on his chest, just above his heart.

This time, James spoke up. "We'll need you to come to Greensboro, probably, to identify them and testify in court. Since you were a victim, we can't have you presiding over the case, so I'm sure we'll shift that privilege to Nathan Gray. But, for the time being, you rest and recuperate. When you're ready to travel, check in with me and I'll let you know what's going on. Matt will be in close contact, too."

"Sounds good."

James filled him in on the details of the boarding house fire the night before. Matt told him how he and Gretchen were going to be cleaning up the boarding house, and they discussed alternative sleeping arrangements for Roger while he stayed in town. James even offered for him to come to Jessup and stay with him or at the plantation.

"Are you leaving town today then?"

"Yes, Olivia is anxious to get back to her children, and I want to get Missus Fields settled in so she can recover without being jostled around any more than is necessary."

"It's too bad you're not staying longer, but I completely understand. So, is it my imagination, or is there something going on between you and Olivia?" Roger asked with a grin.

James laughed. "It's definitely not your imagination. I'm giving her time, though. Her husband has only been gone a few months. I want to make sure she's ready. But," he scratched his cheek and looked sheepishly at both Matt and Roger, "I have asked her to marry me. She said we have to ask the kids."

Both men burst out with amused laughter. "That's wonderful! I'm so happy for you. I hope they say yes. I've never seen you so happy in all the years I've known you, my friend." Matt pounded him on the back and pulled him in for a side hug.

"Thanks. I think they will. They like me, and I adore them. They're great kids. But what about you?"

"James wagged his eyebrows at Matt. "Didn't I see a little spark between you and Gretchen?"

The fierce scowl Matt attempted fell flat, so he grinned. "Well, we've spent quite a bit of time together since that day we interviewed her the last time you were here. By the time we get done cleaning up the boarding house, who knows where we'll stand. She's a special lady, though. I wouldn't mind having more than a friendship with her, but she's just so shy. She seems comfortable with me, though, and I just want to protect her, keep her close, you know?"

"Yep, I know. Funny how God puts situations in our paths that lead us to people we are meant to know. The bandits threatened Olivia the day after I hung my shingle at the end of her street, and she came to me for advice. Maybe the whole reason for the bandits was so that I would let love back into my life. And for you too, Matt. Now, we need to find someone for Roger."

Just then, Daisy waltzed cheerfully into the room to check on her patient and bring his lunch. James noticed how Roger's eyes followed her, and when she touched his chest to check his wound, his face turned red. James leaned over and said to Matt, "Maybe we already did!" Both men laughed, and Roger glared at them and tried to throw a pillow in their direction, causing them to laugh harder. "I guess the bandits did us all a favor!"

"Maybe so. I need to get back to my office and do the job this town pays me to do. Now that I have Roger's statement, I have reports to write and charges to file. Let me know if you need anything, Roger. I'll be back later."

"And I need to talk with Doc and see what other instructions he has for Missus Fields so we can leave soon. Take care, my friend. Come stay with me if you want to."

"I'll let you know. Thanks." Roger's eyes were getting heavy, and Daisy was pushing his lunch tray toward him, but James was sure he was in good hands.

***

On the way home that afternoon, they had decided to go straight to the plantation. James thought that it would be the best place for Missus Fields to recuperate, at least in the beginning. Besides, he had a plan for making it easier for her to be moved from one place to another. She was sure to enjoy the veranda, also.

As he was certain they would, Henry and Catherine welcomed Missus Fields as one of the family. They insisted that she stay with them as long as she wanted to, and they quickly arranged a place for her to sit with her leg propped on pillows in the dining room where people were beginning to assemble for the evening meal. Henry brought in a small table for her food tray to sit on.

As was common at the plantation, several of James's siblings and their families had been invited for dinner, and since Ellie and her family were there, James was happy to introduce Missus Fields to Ellie's husband, John Baker, the local doctor.

James was worried that being surrounded by so much noise and chaos would be too much for the elderly lady, but she seemed to love it. He was also happy to see Frannie and Michael fitting right in with his nieces and nephews. Hopefully soon, they would all be cousins.

After dinner, James walked outside with his Pa. "I have an idea for a chair on wheels to make it easier for Missus Fields to be moved around. Do you want to help me make it?"

"Certainly, lad. I'd be happy to. Tell me about this plan of yours."

They strolled to the barn where woodworking tools were kept while James told him his idea. "It needs wheels so she can be moved by anyone and not have to wait for one of the men to carry her. She's very independent, in case you hadn't noticed." They both laughed. "It should have arms like the wingback chairs, and a way to prop up her leg. Doc gave her crutches to use, but I'm afraid she'll fall again. She could use them to get from the wheeled chair to other chairs or her bed, but she's not to put any weight on that leg until given the approval. What do you think?"

"It's a bonny idea, lad. Let's get started. Here are some pieces of lumber we can use to craft the chair."

It took several hours and many mistakes, but before nightfall, they had a chair on wheels. James was giddy as he brought it into the house to show Missus Fields. Tears spilled from her eyes when she understood what he had done for her.

"Well, forevermore. Come here, dear boy, and let me hug you."

Laughing, he leaned down and accepted her gratitude. Then, turning to Catherine, he said, "Mama, where are we going to have Missus Fields sleep? I'm sure she's getting pretty tired and is probably ready for more of her pain medication."

Missus Fields interrupted. "Young man, we have a long history, you and me. And now you have brought me here to be part of your family while I recover. I think it's high time you stopped calling me 'Missus Fields'. You can call me Agnes, or Granny, since I wasn't blessed to be one." She winked at him, and he hugged her again.

"Alright. Granny it is." His response made her beam.

Several of the children who were within earshot clamored around them. "Do we get to call you Granny, too?"

Her eyes got watery. "I'd be thrilled if you did. I was only blessed with one child, but the Good Lord saw fit to take her when she was young. I like to think I would have been a granny to a few young'uns. But sometimes He gives us gifts we didn't know we needed. Like all of you. Thank you for including me in your home and family, and for letting me call you mine."

The children all took turns hugging her, then ran off to play while the adults fixed up the library with a bed for her. She was delighted to have so much space and thrilled for the bonus of books at her fingertips, but for tonight, she was ready to rest. Olivia stayed with her and helped her get ready for bed.

"When are you going to marry that boy? I've never seen him so happy as I have when he's with you."

Olivia choked and her cheeks turned a delightful shade of pink. "I - um - well -"

Missus Fields laughed. "It's okay. I can see the answer on your face, so you might as well tell me."

Smiling, Olivia complied. "Okay. Yes, he has asked me. Earlier today, in fact. But I didn't answer him yet. I thought we should talk to the children first."

"Pish-posh. A marriage is between two adults, not two adults *and* two children. It's plain to see they adore him. Of course, not many people don't, if you want to know the truth. But he's never so much as shown any interest in anyone until you. So, now, answer me, what are you going to tell him?"

A sweet smile settled on Olivia's lips. "I'm going to tell him yes."

"That's my girl! Go do it. I'm ready to sleep now. Good night, my dear, and thank you for all the ways you've helped me. I like to think you're just like my Susie would have been."

"That's a lovely compliment. Thank you. Good night, Granny." She dropped a kiss on the old lady's soft, wrinkled cheek and went in search of James. She had something important to tell him.

Chapter Twenty-Four

By the time Olivia rejoined the others after seeing to Granny, it had been decided that, since it was late, they would stay at the plantation for the night. All the others had gone to their own homes as most of them lived either on or near the plantation, and Catherine had taken Frannie and Michael upstairs and got them settled.

James thought Olivia looked a little nervous, and decided that a walk outside would do them both some good. He wanted to be alone with her anyway after all the events of the day, and he was still hoping to steal a kiss before the night was over. Watching her, the way she had taken care of Granny, how easily she fit in with his family, he could think of no reason she would refuse his proposal, but until she agreed, his heart would continue to pound.

As he moved close to her, he caught the scent of her hair and skin, a mixture of jasmine and sunshine. The blood pulsed in his veins, and when she smiled at him, he thought the world could end right then and he would be satisfied. "Come on," he whispered to her, "I want to show you something."

"Alright." She accepted the hand he extended to her, and he pulled her out the door leading to the veranda. "Where are we going?"

"It's a surprise." He winked, loving how her cheeks flushed.

His intention had been to just get her away from the house, but now that he had told her he had a surprise for her, he needed to revise his plan. Having grown up on the plantation, he knew all the best places to explore, so his feet reverted back to his childhood as he led her down a path toward the back meadow. He knew there would be wildflowers with all their lovely fragrances, and a wonderful view of the full moon. Maybe he'd get lucky enough to steal a kiss…or two…

When they broke through the trees that had been obscuring the view, Olivia gasped. James watched her face as she took in the scene. A light breeze caused the grass and wildflowers to wave, and a silver stream snaked around rocks making delightful music.

Turning toward him and finding him watching her, she said, "It's lovely, James. So peaceful, so beautiful. I love the scent of the flowers in the air, and the sound of water trickling in the distance. Thank you for bringing me here."

"I have to confess, my motives were a little bit selfish."

One of her eyebrows went up, causing him to laugh. He adored that about her, making him feel younger than his years, but at the same time, chiding his youthful behavior. Gently, he pulled her into his arms, and was relieved when she didn't resist. He nuzzled her ear and felt her shiver, making him glad he was not the only one affected by their closeness.

"James, about this morning." His heart stopped. This was where his hope could die.

"Yes?"

She stepped back away from him, and he allowed her to. "Um, Granny asked me when I was going to marry you since she had never seen you look so happy."

"Okay." He drew out the word, not sure where she was going with this conversation, and not knowing what to expect her to say next. He *thought* he knew her heart, but he wanted to hear it from her.

"I told her you had asked me, but that we needed to talk to the children. She said something that made sense to me."

"What's that, Darlin'?" He spoke softly, desperately wanting to pull her back into his arms and distract her until she said what he wanted to hear. He didn't think his heart could stand it if she refused his proposal. He was sure God had led her to him for the purpose of filling both their lives with a new love.

"She said that marriage is between two adults, not two adults and two children. And of course I knew that, but after losing Peter…" She trailed off for a moment, then continued. "I see how Frannie and

Michael are with you, and I love how you are with them. I'm sure they will be delighted to have you in our family."

He couldn't believe his ears. He realized his heart's desire was about to be fulfilled.

"So, if you still want me - us - then my answer is yes. I would love to be your wife, James"

For a moment, James couldn't move. His eyes roamed over her face, searching to be sure she didn't have any doubts. Then, he hollered with a loud "Whoo - ee!" Not wasting one more minute, he tugged her back into his arms, lifting her up and spinning around while she giggled into his neck.

Slowly, he lowered her until her feet touched the ground, never taking his eyes away from hers. Then, his gaze lowered until he found her mouth. Her tongue darted out in an unconscious effort to moisten her lips, and as if they were magnetized, his lowered until they found hers. The kiss was magical, and he never wanted it to end.

***

The next morning, before driving back into town, James and Olivia gathered Frannie and Michael and told them the news. Of course, their exuberance alerted the rest of the household that something momentous had occurred. James's parents were thrilled to have Olivia, Frannie, and Michael joining the family, and Granny smirked, giving them her "I knew it" look.

After delivering Olivia and the children to their house, James reluctantly left them to visit Ben. He was anxious to find out if the bandits had revealed a motive for their unlawful acts.

"Welcome back, James. And good work back there in Orchard Grove. I guess the timing of everything worked out well, didn't it?"

"Well, I think it took all of us working together to bring those guys in. I'm just glad it's over. What have you been able to find out?"

"Not much yet. Reicher was the only one willing to talk, but I think he's been threatened by the ringleader, so he's pretty tight lipped now, too. Unfortunately, I don't have the space to separate them."

"Hm. We'll get them to talk eventually. Have you notified Judge Gray?"

"No, I figured this is under county jurisdiction."

"Well, there's more to the story, now. They must have been feeling the pinch of us coming down on them, because one of them shot the guy who replaced me on the circuit, Judge Roger Jefferies, and they burned Missus Fields's boarding house. Since Roger is a victim, we can't have him try the case. I'll go over to the telegraph office and send a wire to Nathan. He'll decide how this will be handled."

"They shot a judge?" Ben whistled. "That's pretty bad. Is he okay?"

"He should be fine. Bullet went through the soft tissue of his shoulder. He's sore, but he has a good nurse." James chuckled, and Ben gave him a questioning look. "Doc's daughter works with him, and she was pretty attentive to Roger's care. Might be some love interest going on there, unless I miss my guess."

"Speaking of love interests, how are things with Olivia? Is she still mad at you?"

James laughed. "No, she reluctantly agreed to go with me, and I kept my mouth shut for a good long while. Then she opened up and told me why she had reacted the way she did. We talked a long time after that. She was staying with Missus Fields that first night and insisted on having a bed made up on the couch just outside her room in case she needed something. I can't tell you how glad I am that she was right there, because when the fire broke out, she was able to get everyone inside out of the house without injury. That happened not long after Matt and I ran to the saloon where Roger had been shot. I'm thinking these jokers took advantage of the distraction to go set the fire. We found a whiskey bottle and evidence of an accelerant, like kerosene."

"Yeah, these guys are going to be put away for a while."

"I can't tell you how relieved I was to hear that you were patrolling the streets around Olivia's house.

They probably would have burned it next. Between you and Matt, you did a great job. Thank you."

"I'm glad I was in the right place at the right time. I was on my way back to the office when I heard hoofbeats coming, so I just waited. Seemed unusual, with the lateness of the hour."

"I'll be glad when we get them put away in prison, but first we need to find out why they were doing this."

"Let's go have a talk with them. I'll bring in Reicher for you to talk to. Sound good?"

"Let's do it."

***

The following week, James and Ben escorted the four prisoners to Greensboro to stand trial in Nathan Gray's courtroom. The lawmen were not inclined to treat them especially well since they had refused every request to tell the truth, but being men of integrity, they were not abusive, only firm in their handling. Still, they were more than happy to hand them over to the guards at the courthouse and meet with Matt and Roger, who had arrived just moments before.

Roger was wearing a sling to help him remember not to use his left arm more than necessary. He was still experiencing pain but was healing nicely from the gunshot wound. They thought they knew which man had shot him from what the saloon owner had told Matt, but if Roger could identify him, the sentencing would be more accurate. James also suspected that the man who shot Roger was also the one responsible for the fire at the boarding house.

Before the trial began, Judge Gray called the four men into his chambers.

"I know it's not regular practice to do this, but James and Roger are colleagues, and you other men are with them. We can't talk about the case, but I just wanted to visit a little before the day gets started. First, let me tell you that I'm glad this puzzling case is over, and that you're still toes above the ground, Roger. When I heard you'd been shot, I was really worried."

Roger laughed. "Believe me, I'm glad my toes are still above ground, too! I wasn't sure there for a while."

"Ah, but we suspect he has something to live for, don't you?" Matt elbowed him and chuckled. Roger tried to look menacing but couldn't help the smile that crept onto his face.

James joined in the laughter. "Ah, tell us more! A lot can happen in a week."

Ben jumped in. "You should know. You left town with your lady mad at you and came back smiling like a madman."

"Matt might have some answering to do, too."

Judge Gray cut in with a twinkle in his eye and a smirk on his face. "Alright, gentlemen. All of you start confessing. James, you first."

James's look of surprise and mock outrage caused all of them to laugh. "Alright, I'm not afraid to admit it. I fell hard for the lovely Missus Martin, and next week she will become my wife. You all are invited to the wedding at the plantation." Everyone congratulated him and patted his shoulder while he smiled his thanks. "Matt? You go next."

Matt cleared his throat a couple of times, then said, "Gretchen has agreed to let me officially court her. We've been working on Missus Fields' place, cleaning it up so we can rebuild the kitchen. James, we'd like to offer to buy it from her, but she'd be welcome to live out her days there with us. What do you think?"

"I think that would be wonderful. Once she's back on her feet, she can decide, but we'd like for her to stay with us, if she will. She's asked us all to call her Granny, and the kids just adore her. They never had any grandparents, so they're really enjoying her and my parents."

"I'm planning on stopping by to see her on my way home. Maybe I'll mention it and let her start thinking about it. No need to rush her decision, though. Okay, Roger, your turn."

Roger looked a little uncomfortable being put on the spot, but after a little teasing from the others, he finally admitted, "I had the most delightful nurse after I got shot. She's vibrant and sweet, a genuine ray of sunshine. I'm not sure where we'll end up, but we're going to keep seeing each other - when I'm in Orchard Grove, at least. I'm not sure how to make it work, but we'll try."

"That's great, Roger. If it's in God's plan for you, it will work out. He'll show you the way." Nathan always had a way of shedding light on everything, and as he looked around at these young men, he smiled and nodded as though he saw the bigger picture for each of them. "Now, Ben, we haven't yet heard from you. Any love in your life?"

Ben was so quick to answer that he almost choked on his words, making them all laugh. "NO! No, I don't have time for women. I like my life just the way it is."

Just then, there was a knock on the door. Nathan yelled, "Enter", and a lovely young lady came in to hand the judge a note. James elbowed Matt and Roger and nodded toward Ben, indicating they should look in his direction. Ben hadn't taken his eyes off the girl, and when she made eye contact with him and smiled, his face turned red. The three men couldn't contain their laughter.

As the door closed behind the girl, Nathan saw what they had, then, and smiled. "Ben, would you like me to introduce you to Abigail? She's my wife's assistant. It would be no trouble at all. I understand she is unattached. Lovely girl."

Ben looked like he wanted to run, but after a few moments, he gave in and joined in the laughter. He even agreed to an introduction later.

"Well, boys, this has been a lot of fun for an old man like me, but duty calls. It's almost time for court. I'll see you all in a few minutes."

Chapter Twenty-Five

The prisoners were brought into the courtroom, each of them wearing a different expression, varying from contrite to angry. James watched each of them closely, as was his practice. One by one, they would be questioned by the judge, and he wondered which one of them would break down and tell everything.

"State your names."

"Aerick Reicher"

"Oscar Reynolds"

"Roy Franklin"

"Louis Beaufort"

"You four men are charged with extorting property from widowed women. In addition, you are charged with two counts of attempted murder, and one count of arson. Did you do these things?" Judge Gray's authoritative voice caused most criminals to crumble, but one man in particular looked at him with contempt and refused to answer.

Aerick Reicher started to speak, but the contemptuous one elbowed him, and he shushed.

"Alright, then, we'll do this the hard way. See, when you admit you did wrong, things go a lot easier for you. Might want to start learning that lesson now. So, since no one wants to admit they did anything, I'm going to interview you one by one, right here in front of everyone present. Mister Reicher, you're first. No, don't look at any of your friends. You can help yourself a lot by being honest and telling me what I need to know. Is that clear?"

"Yes, sir."

"How long have you been part of this gang?"

"Three years, I reckon."

"And what is your job?"

"I been keeping track of properties that come available and watching out for deputies."

"But weren't *you* a deputy, Mister Reicher?" Nathan's sarcasm made James's lips twitch.

He had the good sense to look ashamed. "Um, yessir."

"How did you get sworn in if you're one of this gang?"

"Wasn't exactly forthcomin' with everything, I reckon."

"Like what?"

"Like how I got the property where I lived, and what I do."

"What were your answers?"

"I said I bought the place as it was abandoned, and kept cattle. Lots of pasture and so on. But I did live there. We all did."

"Was the place abandoned?"

"Er, not when we acquired it."

"And did you raise cattle?"

"Um, no."

"Alright, so you lied, didn't you?"

"I reckon I did, yessir."

"How *did* you get the property, Mister Reicher?"

"Well, um, see..."

"Get to the point!" Nathan slammed his fist on the desk, and Reicher jumped.

"We took it from a widow lady."

"Exactly how do you "take" property from someone?"

"Um, we hear of places where the husband died, then we tell the widow we'll come fix up her place in exchange for a roof and food."

"Then what?"

"I don't rightly know what, sir. I never saw it go that far."

"What do you mean?"

"Well, we have papers we want 'em to sign. A couple of 'em signed, but most just run off, so we take over the property."

"What happened with the ones who signed?"

"Roy goes and just keeps stayin' till the lady leaves. It's in the contract that if they abandon the property, it becomes ours."

"But these contracts aren't exactly legal, are they?"

"I dunno."

"Hrmph. So, each of you have specific jobs? Yours is finding the places, and Roy outstays his welcome. What about the others?"

"Louis charms 'em into signing. He's the one who talks to them first, usually. And Oscar plans everything and scares them into leaving if they don't sign."

"That's quite an elaborate operation. Why are you boys doing this? And why are you targeting widow ladies as your victims?"

"Well, our boss wants access to a whole lot of land through here, but he don't want to spend a lot of money. Told us to be creative and just get it done, so that's the plan Oscar decided on."

"So, there's someone else who's paying you to do this "job" for him? Who is it?"

"I don't know his name, sir."

"Well, what *do* you know?" James could almost hear Nathan rolling his eyes.

Reicher looked nervously at Oscar but forged ahead with his confession. "All I know is he's a British lord. He owns a few merchant ships on the coast as well as some silver mines up in the mountains"

Judge Gray's eyebrows disappeared into his hairline, and the chins of James, Matt, Ben and Roger dropped almost into their laps. Nathan tented his fingers in front of him as he thought for a moment. "What's he planning to do with the properties?"

"Build a rail to get the silver to his ships."

Gasps and chatter sounded around the courtroom, but Nathan didn't even put a stop to it. Instead, he called for a recess and beckoned James and the others to come with him. He needed time for his mind to absorb this information, and he wanted the input from the other men.

When they reached his chambers, they found Nathan pacing. James had never seen him this rattled before. He came to a stop behind his chair, hands braced on the back. He looked up at them, shaking his head.

"I can't believe what I just heard. They're trying to build a secret railway to steal the silver that belongs here in North Carolina. Probably planning to ship it back to jolly old England. I'll not allow that to happen in my lifetime!" A vein in Nathan's forehead was pulsing.

"Matt and I put a map on the wall in his office when we were first learning about this activity, and put pins in places we had heard were taken, but until we saw the papers from Missus Fields, we had no reason to question anyone. The pins didn't make any sense, though. There wasn't a strong enough pattern. And Olivia's place makes no sense at all."

"Yeah, I was thinking about that, too. Why her place? At best, it's way out of the way from the rest of them." Matt was scratching his head.

Ben spoke up. "Probably need to ask them that question."

Nathan looked up. "I plan to, believe me."

"Might be something specific to that property that they want," Roger suggested.

"Mhmm. Could be. Alright, do any of you have any other thoughts?"

Matt asked, "Do we need to call in the army to stop this British scoundrel? Also, where else are they doing this? Reicher says he's been with them for three years. How long has this been going on? How many properties have they stolen?"

"Let's go find out. Thanks for your input, gentlemen."

They filed back into the courtroom, and the prisoners were returned to their seats in front of the judge.

"Alright, Mister Reicher, since you've been cooperating, I hope you don't mind answering more questions. Believe me, I'll have plenty of questions for the rest of you, but you can just wait your turn. Now, Mister Reicher, please explain to me how long all of this activity has been going on."

"Um, I'm not rightly sure, sir. Longer than I've been with them."

"Do you have any idea how many properties have been, shall we say, acquired?"

"I've only worked in this region, and since I've been working with these men, we've acquired twelve successfully."

"How many 'unsuccessfully'?"

"Two."

"Let me guess. One is the boarding house in Orchard Grove."

"Er, yessir."

"Why go after that place?"

"It's within the boundaries of where he wanted land."

"So, start with one place in town and eventually wipe out the whole town? Is that part of the plan?"

"I don't know. I don't think so."

"And what about Missus Martin's place in Jessup?"

James's gaze on the men intensified.

"Well, um, there's something there we need."

"Go on."

"We have a map with coordinates marked. I don't really know exactly what it is, maybe Oscar does."

Oscar growled and shot a menacing look first to Reicher, then to James and the others. James figured he was angry for getting caught. Roger leaned over and whispered to James, "Oscar is the one who shot me. I remember seeing the scar on his forehead."

Nathan continued. "Alright, we'll come back to that then. Can you describe your territory? How much area is in your region?"

"From the mines to Greensboro, and from the northern border of North Carolina to approximately fifty miles south."

Judge Gray whistled. "That's a mighty big territory. What happens when you can't get property that connects to make this rail line happen?"

"Um, well, er, we have to find a way to make them connect."

"Whatever it takes?"

"Yessir." James scowled, wondering how many women had become widows "accidentally".

"Is there another outfit similar to yours working the eastern half of the state?"

"I reckon so, but I don't know for sure."

"Who shot Judge Jefferies?"

"Sir?"

"I'm sure you heard me. Who shot the man in the saloon ten days ago?"

Reicher had the sense to turn pale. "Uh, that was Oscar"

Oscar started to jump to his feet, turning toward Reicher as he did so, fist clenched and growling. "Sit down, Mister Reynolds! I had to ask someone who I believed would tell me the truth. Your behavior so far leads me to believe you won't answer a single thing honestly, but know this. There are things I already know as fact, so when you lie to me, I'll add years onto your sentence. Got it?"

After a stare down, Oscar reluctantly gave a brief nod. Judge Gray maintained eye contact long enough to send a message, then returned to Reicher.

"Alright, Mister Reicher. Thank you for your answers. You may take your seat. Now, Mister Reynolds. I have one question for you. What is it about Missus Martin's property that interests your employer?"

Oscar stared at the floor, then at the wall behind the judge, then to the opposite corner of the room without speaking.

"I'm waiting, Mister Reynolds. You will answer me. Now!" Again, Nathan pounded the desk with his fist. All the prisoners except Oscar flinched, but the command did its job.

"There's a box buried there we were supposed to find and bring in."

"What sort of box?"

"It has papers in it that they buried when the war broke out in these parts."

"So, documents important to the British, or to your employer?"

"Well, they told him to get them since he has the ships and all."

"Is it connected with this rail line he wants to build?"

"Nah, but since we're in this region, he wanted us to find it. It was just convenient that her old man got his self killed."

"Why try to steal her property then? Why not just get permission to find it?"

"Cuz we don't know exactly where it is. Might take a bit to find it."

"So, stealing the house would make it easier because no one would question you digging up the yard?"

"I guess."

"How do you know it's on that property?"

"Got a map with coordinates. Matches her place."

"Where is this map?"

"At our hideout."

"You will give me detailed instructions on how to find the map, and Sheriff O'Connor will see that it is brought to me, then we will continue this. Just one more question. Why did you burn the boarding house?"

"Old lady snitched. Louis didn't get the papers back from her and she told the sheriff."

"You don't sound remorseful at all."

Oscar glared. Nathan had had enough.

"Take the prisoners back to their cells and get me that information immediately. Make sure they are in separate areas so they can't talk to each other. We will resume at a later date."

James, Matt, Ben and Roger followed Nathan back to his chambers again. Something was bothering James that he wanted to talk about with them.

"This Englishman is expecting something to be brought from the land where Olivia's house sits. With them locked up, what's to say he doesn't send someone else to look for it? Olivia and the children are still in danger."

"I believe you could be right, James. Ben, do you have someone keeping an eye on them today?"

"Not specifically, but Colin is covering for me. I'll run over to the telegraph office and send him a wire, let him know to watch." Ben rushed out the door while James fumed. He didn't like leaving his family alone today anyway, and now that there might still be danger for them had him pacing around Nathan's chambers like a caged tiger.

Since the trial wouldn't continue until after Matt retrieved the map from the gang's hideout, they would be heading home once Ben returned. Each of the men were quietly thinking about what had transpired over the last couple of hours.

James had never heard of such things happening before, and even with his experience as a judge, he was glad this one was in Nathan's courtroom. He wanted to lock all of them up for a very long time, but it was pivotal that they found out what was so important on Olivia's property. It was also important to know the name of the Englishman ordering this illegal activity.

Maybe they could have him banned from American soil.

Suddenly, Ben burst into Nathan's office. "Sorry to barge in like this, but no sooner had I sent the wire to Colin than I got one back saying he caught a couple of guys in Olivia's carriage house. They had made holes in different places in the backyard, which they tried to fill back in. Fortunately, she and the children had been gone, and when they returned, she felt like something was off. Instead of taking her rig into the carriage house, she went straight to my office where she reported it to Colin. It seems they found the box, and Colin has it in the safe."

James sagged into the nearest chair. "Hallelujah! Thank the Lord my family is now safe, and we don't need to wait for the map to finish the trial. But I still want to know what's in that box."

A chorus of "Me, too" went around the room. Nathan leaned back in his chair, hands clasped behind his head. "I think I'll let these jokers stew for a few days, but we can get all this wrapped up before your wedding, James. Why don't you all go home and rest easy for now? Let's finish this next Wednesday. Ben, you and your deputy bring that box with you when you bring the other two prisoners."

It was a much happier group that departed the courthouse than what entered it earlier in the day. Since Roger was still recovering from his wound, James insisted he come to Jessup to stay with him, at least until the trial was over. Matt said he would be stopping at the plantation to visit Missus Fields, and Nathan gathered his wife from her desk outside his office and declared they were going home early for a change.

Chapter Twenty-Six

On Wednesday, the courtroom was crowded. It had been such an unusual case that, with so many lives affected, interest was at an all-time high. There were so many spectators that it was standing room only. Olivia, Henry and Catherine had accompanied James, and Gretchen came with Matt from Orchard Grove. Missus Fields had wanted to come, but since she was still in a good amount of pain, Catherine had persuaded her to stay home.

When Ben and Colin brought the newest prisoners into the courtroom, surprise flared in the eyes of the bandits. It was evident they were acquainted. The question in James's mind was how well they knew one another. He hoped Nathan would ask that question.

Nathan entered the courtroom and resumed the trial.

"Mister Reynolds, we'll pick back up where we left off last week. You did give accurate instructions for finding the map, so that's in your favor. When were you planning to go back to Missus Martin's place to look for the buried treasure?" Snickers broke out across the courtroom.

Oscar scowled, but eventually answered. "We was gonna look the night they caught us, but we weren't carrying the map, so we was gonna come back later after the heat was off of us."

"Do you know these two men that Sheriff Richardson and Deputy MacKay brought in today?"

Oscar's mouth formed a straight, tight line.

"You might as well answer. We already know the truth."

Glaring at Judge Gray, he hesitated, then gave in. "Yeah, I've seen them with the boss."

"Right." He drew out the word. "The English lord you never met. What was his name again?" Nathan stroked his chin as he baited the man.

Oscar cleared his throat, and Louis looked like he wanted to answer the question, but instead of saying something, he elbowed Oscar. James hid a smile. The men seemed to finally be getting the message that truth would win.

"Name's Lord Albert Fitzsimmon. He owns a fleet of ships and several mines."

"Alright. Thank you, Mister Reynolds. One more question. Do you know what is in the box you were sent to recover?"

"No. We was just told to get it and turn it over to him."

"Okay. You may be seated. We're going to skip over to the newcomers, now. Stand and tell me your names."

"Leo Wadsworth."

"Ernest Clement."

"Would one of you please tell me what you were doing digging holes in Missus Martin's yard?"

"We was sent by My Lord to retrieve the box." The man's British accent was heavy and lacked the polish of nobility.

"Are you referring to this Fitzsimmon character?"

"Quite right."

"And did you find the box, Mister Wadsworth?"

"Aye, we did. 'Twas buried in the floor of the stables, it was."

"What is in the box?"

"Don't know, m'lor - er, sir. Didn't have time ta look 'fore it was ripped outta me hands that was bein' shackled."

"Don't you have any idea what it is that was so important that someone needed it found?"

"Jus' some papers, 'tis all I know."

"Do the papers belong to this lord Fitzsimmon?"

"He was told to find 'em. Somethin' that was buried when the war broke out."

Nathan sighed. He called a recess and invited James, Roger, Matt, Ben and Colin to his chambers. Ben brought the box along with him.

"Alright, once and for all, let's discover what's in this box," he muttered. The lock on the box was rusty, but Colin had a screwdriver in his pocket that enabled them to force it open. Five necks stretched to look over Nathan's shoulder. With a creak and a groan, the lid swung open revealing several certificates showing where multiple chests of gold were hidden. When they realized what they had in their hands, they looked around the room at each other in complete amazement.

"Well, I'll be!" Nathan's face broke out in a huge smile. "This is huge, boys. Do you have any idea what I think this is?"

They each looked around at the others, heads shaking. "You seem to know. What is it?"

"About ten years or so before the war broke out, a British ship went missing. There was speculation that the Brits sank it because they were carrying a lot of money that they didn't want getting into the hands of the colonists. Some said they stole their own money and hid it somewhere, and I'm thinking they were right. It's all laid out right here!"

Whistles of surprise sounded around the room. "So, what do we do now?"

"I'll have to turn this over to the Attorney General. If this is indeed that money, they will take steps to press charges against Britain. I will insist that this Fitzsimmon is charged with larceny, specifically for the properties he's acquired illegally, and that his shipping company be barred from trading in American waters. I'll see what I can do to remove the mines from his possession, also." He stood up and smiled at each of them. "Boys, you all have done a terrific job of bringing down these criminals. Who knew it was going to be such an intricately woven scheme. On behalf of the United States of America, thank you! All that's left now is the sentencing."

Soon after, they all filed back into the courtroom, smiles on their faces. The friends and family who had come to support them looked at them questioningly.

James draped his arm around Olivia and whispered in her ear. Matt took Gretchen's hand in his, squeezing gently, then sent her a wink and a smile. A low murmur was heard across the courtroom as spectators whispered questions to one another, wondering why everyone was smiling.

Nathan addressed the prisoners. "First, all of you are going to prison. Some of your crimes are more heinous than others, so the length of your sentences will vary. Mister Reicher, your testimony was most helpful, while yours, Mister Reynolds, along with the evil nature of your actions, will be longer. Mister Clement, I want you to write a telegram to Mister Fitzsimmon, letting him know that the box has been retrieved and that no more searching of Missus Martin's property will be necessary. Let him know he will be contacted with details regarding the box shortly." He then assigned the appropriate length sentence to each man.

"Now, I'm sure everyone here is wondering what was in the box. I am not at liberty to discuss the details, but we are confident the documents inside the box are directly related to British piracy dating to the years prior to the Revolution. They will be turned over to the Attorney General for resolution. I'm sorry, I cannot tell you more at this time until my suspicions are verified. At that time, I'm certain you can read about it in the newspapers. Court is adjourned."

James was anxious to introduce his beloved to his friend and mentor, so they made their way to Nathan's office. Missus Gray came in, also, bringing a bottle of champagne to celebrate the conclusion of the trial and to toast the happy couple. After they visited for a short time, James hugged them both and made sure they planned to attend their wedding in two days, then he took Olivia's hand and led her to their team that would return them home to Jessup.

***

Olivia was surprisingly calm the morning of her wedding. She couldn't wait to become James's wife:

Missus MacKay. It had a nice ring to it, and she couldn't stop smiling.

She and the children had stayed at the plantation the night before, and the children were as excited as she was. Michael was running all over, getting in the way of the preparations, and she had to keep reminding him to slow down and talk quieter. Granny Fields refused to allow Michael to push her chair for her. She said he was a dangerous driver and she didn't want to break her neck next.

Frannie walked around with her head in the clouds. You would have thought it was her wedding, the way she was carrying on. Olivia laughed as the girl waltzed to imaginary music all over the hallways and in the parlors. Henry and Catherine just chuckled, enjoying having them all in the house.

The household staff had done a beautiful job decorating. The ceremony was to be in the large parlor, then there would be dancing on the veranda. Everyone worked together all morning, putting finishing touches on the house. Aromas coming from the kitchen were making them all hungry.

After a light lunch, it was time to get ready for the wedding. Catherine had helped Olivia create her ensemble for the day, and she couldn't wait to put it on. What would James think? She hoped he would like her dress. She had so enjoyed working with his mother on it.

Before getting dressed herself, she helped Frannie get ready. Frannie's dress was a pink calico, fitting her slim form loosely, giving her a little room to grow without it being too big. They talked while Olivia brushed the long, blond hair that matched her own. Olivia noticed a hint of reservation in Frannie's eyes.

"What's going on in that mind of yours, Sweetie? Is everything alright?"

"Yeah, I guess so."

"Tell me what you're worried about."

Frannie fidgeted with her fingers for a few moments, then met her mother's eyes in the mirror.

"Do you still love Papa?"

Olivia almost dropped the brush she held in her hand.

"Honey, I will always love your Papa. Nothing will change that. Ever."

"But how can you love him *and* Mister MacKay? How can you be married to them both?"

How was she supposed to answer this in a way a child could understand? She hesitated before answering.

"Darling, your Papa and I loved each other very much. It was our intention to spend many years together, growing old together, watching you and Michael fall in love and have families of your own. But it wasn't meant to be. Part of my heart will always belong to your Papa. But God did something really special for me. He made my love grow so much that I could find love with another man. I'm not still married to your father, because he's no longer here, and that makes it okay for me to be married to James. Does that make sense?"

Frannie nodded, but Olivia knew more questions were coming.

"Will Mister MacKay expect us to call him Papa?"

Olivia smiled at the formal name. In a matter of a few hours, they would be a family. It would not do for her children to keep calling him "Mister MacKay"!

"No, darling, he won't expect you to call him Papa, but I think we need to find a new name for him besides Mister MacKay."

Frannie giggled when she realized how silly that would sound when they would all be living in the same house. "I guess we could ask him what he'd like to be called."

"I think that's a wonderful idea. You know, he does not ever want you to forget your father. We will both work at helping you remember everything about him."

"I know." She chewed on her lip. "I'm glad he's going to be part of our family."

"Me too, sweetie. He's been a gift from God."

Olivia pulled her daughter in for a tight hug, then asked her to go check on Michael just as Catherine's personal maid, Bessie, came in to help Olivia get dressed. Olivia had learned in a short amount of time that Bessie loved to talk while she worked, but Olivia enjoyed it. She was a dear woman with a kind heart. She told stories about James as a child, making Olivia laugh about his silly antics and her heart swell with love over sweet anecdotes.

When she was ready, Olivia sat in the chair by the window to wait until it was time for the ceremony. Her heart was happier than it had been since Peter's death, and she took a moment to thank God for helping her through such a painful time, and for bringing this wonderful man into her life.

Lord, thank you for always providing our needs, even when we don't know what those are. You sent James when I was frightened and alone, and you used him to remind me of Your love for me, and I will always be grateful. Help me to be a good wife to him.

A soft knock sounded on the bedroom door, and she rose to answer it. Catherine asked if she could come in for a moment, as it was nearly time to go downstairs. She was carrying a small basket filled with freshly cut flowers and handed it to Olivia.

"I had the children cut these for you. I thought you might like to carry them in a basket rather than tied with a ribbon, but if you'd rather, we can tie them up quickly."

"No, this is beautiful. I love it. Thank you."

"Are you ready? Everyone is here, and I know one man who can't wait to see you." Catherine's kind smile was accompanied by her twinkling eyes.

Olivia laughed. "I can't wait to see him, either. I'm ready."

Catherine went ahead, then Olivia descended the stairs to where Henry was waiting to escort her to the ceremony. When they rounded the corner into the large room that was filled with family and friends, her eyes sought James, and their gazes locked. She smiled brilliantly, and she could see a sheen in his eyes as he swallowed a few times before finding his own smile.

His eyes never left her. She was breathtaking. Her dress was a cornflower blue, the exact shade of her eyes, cut in a flattering style that was modest but alluring. Her honey-blond hair was gathered at her nape, with a tiny braid circling her crown. Her long tresses hung in ringlets down her back, and flowers were woven throughout.

When she reached where he stood, his father placed a sweet kiss on her cheek and welcomed her to the family, then placed her hand in James's. Somehow, they made it through the ceremony, and he must have said all the right things, because then the pastor told him he could kiss his bride. He had to reign in the exuberance, at least for now, but apparently, no one was fooled, because the whole room erupted in laughter.

James had the overwhelming urge to lift Olivia over his shoulder and run. He wanted nothing more than to be alone with his wife. *Wife!* He never expected to be blessed in this way again, but every day since he'd met Olivia, he thanked the Lord for putting her on his doorstep that morning.

Since it would have been frowned upon to steal his wife and run, he settled for taking her hand, drawing it through his arm, and retreating to the back of the room where they could slip out onto the veranda before everyone came around to congratulate them. He pulled her into some shadows and tugged her into his arms.

"Hello, wife." He smiled, then lowered his head for another kiss. The one that concluded the ceremony hadn't been enough, and he wanted more.

"Hello, husband." Her arms snaked up around his neck and she took the initiative to pull him in for yet another kiss.

"You are so beautiful today. You are always beautiful, but today is my favorite, since it's the day you officially became mine. I love you, Olivia MacKay."

"I love you, James MacKay. I never expected to find love again, but I'm so glad I did."

Just then, their private moment was interrupted by a hurricane the size of Michael. They both laughed, and Olivia told James what Granny had said earlier. A moment later, Frannie came alongside them.

James drew both children in for a hug, then said, "I want to thank you both for letting me join your family. I promise to take really good care of both of you and your mama. I love you all so very much, and I'm glad God gave you to me."

"Are you our Pa now?" Michael asked, scrunching his nose in uncertainty.

James's eyes went wide, as he looked first at Michael, then at Olivia. They hadn't talked about this. "Well, Michael, your Pa will always be your Pa, but since he isn't here any longer, God gave me the privilege of helping take care of some of his jobs. One of those things is to be *like* a Pa to you. I'll be here for you always. I'll answer your questions and teach you what you need to know to become the man you were meant to be. Is that alright with you?"

Michael flung his little body into James's arms. "Yep! It's better than alright. Now I have two Pa's. What are we supposed to call you now?"

"I don't know. What do you think you should call me?"

Frannie spoke for the first time during that whole exchange. "Well, we can't keep calling you Mister MacKay," she grinned.

James burst out laughing and hugged her. "No, I don't suppose so. Why don't we just think about it for a while. Meanwhile, you can call me James, okay?"

That seemed to satisfy them for now, and they ran off to find their new cousins. Olivia smiled into his eyes. "You were wonderful, the way you answered him. Frannie and I had a little discussion on that same topic earlier. She was concerned that I didn't love her papa anymore. I told her God expanded my heart to love both of you. She seemed fine with that."

"That's a great way to explain it, too. You're a wonderful mother. I love watching you with them. Of course, I just love watching you." He winked at her, causing her cheeks to flush. "Come on, Missus MacKay, let's greet our guests so I can dance with my wife in a little while."

The next few hours flew by as they enjoyed visiting with their guests and dancing to the music played by the stringed instruments, but the best part of all was when James pulled Olivia away from everyone else.

"Sweetheart, are you ready to go? Since the children are staying with Ellie's family for a couple of days, I'm ready to have you all to myself. What do you say?"

"Let's say goodbye to the children, then I'm all yours."

"I like the sound of that." Olivia laughed when he wagged his eyebrows at her. "Let's go!"

Epilogue

About a year later

James paced up and down the hallway. His palms were wet, and sweat beaded on his forehead. He stopped outside the bedroom door, pressing his ear against the wood. Suddenly, the door opened, and Ellie emerged. She took in his haunted look, shook her head, and shoved him out of her way.

"How is she? Is everything alright?"

"Everything is fine. Why don't you go outside and get some fresh air."

"I can't. I need to stay right here."

"You realize it could be a while, right?"

"I need to stay here. She needs me."

"I think it's *you* who needs *her*," she muttered. Then she laid a gentle hand on his arm and spoke softly.

"James, she'll be fine. The baby is in the correct position, and the heartbeat is strong. I know it's hard not to, but worrying will not change anything. John will let you know if there's something to worry about, okay?"

Absentmindedly, he nodded, then resumed his pacing. Anytime the bedroom door opened, he tried to get in, but Granny was always there, pushing him back out into the hallway. He didn't understand why he wasn't allowed to be in there. It seemed only right that he be allowed to hold her hand and comfort her through her pain. After all, this was his child, too. He needed to be there with her. He couldn't stand knowing she was suffering, and he was helpless to do anything about it.

More time passed. It seemed like several hours, but the sun was still bright outside. His parents had taken Frannie and Michael, along with John and Ellie's children, to the plantation to play with the new kittens that afternoon, and he was grateful for that. He didn't want them to see him in this state; he didn't want to frighten them. They were too young and impressionable, and he didn't trust his ability to remain calm.

After losing both Victoria and baby John, of course he was concerned that it would happen again. He remembered how terrified he was when he first learned that Olivia was carrying his child. He had avoided sleeping in their room for several days, but she finally convinced him that he could neither cause nor prevent a recurrence of what happened before. She insisted that she needed him to be the husband she married, and that life comes with good *and* bad. They both understood that. He just didn't think he would be able to survive if he lost her.

A loud cry came from the direction of their bedroom, and he ran back to the door. This time, he didn't hesitate; he barged right in, running to her side.

"James, you can't be in here." Ellie attempted to intercept him on his way to Olivia's side.

"No! Stay here, James, I need you. Please!" Olivia's grip on his hand made the decision for him. He was not leaving this room anytime soon. Another wave of pain washed over her, and his fingers turned white from her crushing grasp.

John and Ellie exchanged looks, and John said, "Alright, he can stay, as long as he stays out of the way. Olivia, with the next contraction, I want you to push as hard as you can. James, get behind her shoulders to give her leverage. Here we go."

James shifted behind Olivia as John had said, and soon he was feeling her tension with the contraction. He stroked her shoulder with one hand, her fingers with the other, and kissed her temple, whispering words of encouragement in her ear. The next thing he knew, she was relaxing against him, sweat beading on her forehead, and breathing hard. He looked up to find his brother-in-law lifting a wet, purple infant and putting it in the blanket Ellie was holding.

"Doctor, why isn't the baby crying?" Olivia's panicked voice brought him back into focus, but they need not have worried, because just then, the child's outraged squall let them know that those lungs worked just fine. Olivia looked up at James, and he held her close, kissing her with tears streaming down his face.

"Would you like to hold your son, big brother?" Ellie said with a smile.

"It's a boy? Darling, did you hear that? It's a boy!"

"Let me see him." Smiling, Olivia gently pulled down the side of the blanket that was around the baby's face. They marveled over the miracle they had created, and James whispered a prayer of thanksgiving for keeping his wife and son safe.

After John and Ellie finished cleaning up the birthing area, they stepped out of the room, with Granny following close behind, leaving James and Olivia alone with their new son.

"What shall we name him?" Olivia looked at James with contentment and adoration in her eyes.

"I think we should call him William, in honor of your father. William Isaac MacKay."

"That's perfect."

***

Later that night, Henry and Catherine brought Frannie and Michael home. The children had been warned that the baby might not have been born yet, and they were not to go charging into their mother's room. However, they were met in the parlor by a smiling Granny.

"Granny! Is the baby here yet?" Frannie had been beside herself with excitement over the pending birth of the newest member of the family. This was even better than a new litter of kittens! She wanted to learn everything she could about being a good big sister and had peppered her mother with questions over the past several weeks.

"Why don't you go upstairs and knock on the bedroom door. If your mama's awake, maybe you can ask her for yourself." Granny chuckled and shook her head as she watched Michael tear up the stairs ahead of his sister. After the children were gone, she turned to Catherine and Henry, whose faces were etched with concern. They knew James had been worrying about this day throughout the entire pregnancy.

"Is everything alright?" Catherine asked softly.

"Yes, everything is perfect. Poor James wore a path on that rug up there in the hallway. He ended up barging in, and no one was going to remove him from the room." She laughed, while Catherine gasped and Henry chuckled. "Doc let him stay as long as he promised to keep out of the way. His presence seemed to have a calming effect on Olivia, so it worked out alright in the end. Olivia is doing very well, and the baby is happy and healthy."

"That's wonderful news! We'll give them some time with the children, then go meet our newest grandchild."

Meanwhile, upstairs, Frannie and Michael had been invited in to meet their new baby brother. Frannie was itching to touch him, and Michael just stared at him with wonder.

"He's so small. How long until he can play with me?"

James laughed. "We need to give him time to grow a while. Remember how tiny your little cousin, Eli, was when he was first born? He has grown a lot, but there's much he still needs to learn before he can play with the big kids. Same for William. It might seem like he isn't growing at all, but one day, probably in about a year, he'll start to walk a little bit. In about two years, he should be able to run, but it might be a few more before he can play ball with you."

Michael crossed his arms across his chest and frowned. "That's too long."

Everyone laughed, and Frannie finally asked, "Mama, Daddy, can I hold him?" Olivia watched as James helped arrange the baby comfortably in their daughter's arms. Then she invited Michael up onto the bed beside her, pulling him in for a hug.

"Just be patient, Michael. God gave you this little brother, and that's an important job for you. For right now, we will just love him, and watch him grow, and help him learn new things."

Michael and Frannie exchanged a look. Then Michael said, "I'm glad we have a new brother." He leaned over Olivia's lap to touch the baby's hand, giggling when the tiny fist grabbed his finger.

"Me too," Frannie added. Then, talking softly to her new brother, she said, "You're going to love it here, William. We have the best Mama and Daddy ever." Then, looking around at each person, she said, "I love our family!" and she brushed a kiss over the downy, soft head of the baby in her arms.

Tears pooled in James's eyes as he met Olivia's own watery ones over Michael's head. They were, indeed, blessed.

…to be continued in future generations.

A Note from the Author

Thank you, dear Reader, for taking the time to read this story. I hope you enjoyed it!

Thank you to all who have helped me put this project together. To my "team" (Diana, Sue, and Linda) who read the early drafts and gave reactions, suggestions and advice for grammar, content and clarity, and to the many others who cheered me on and pushed me to finalize the story because they can't wait to read it, your encouragement is so valuable to me. And to Linda for another beautiful cover: in spite of the challenges you face in making it happen, your efforts are so appreciated.

I was inspired to create these stories after my husband's passing. He had researched his family ancestry and I thought that the legacy should somehow be passed to our children (as well as all members of the Kinney clan) Some of the ideas are based loosely on truth: the family came from Scotland originally, and we are pretty certain that someone participated in at least one battle with the British during the Revolutionary War. Some of the character names are borrowed from the family tree, but dates and circumstances are purely fiction.

Just a bit about me: I never knew I had a passion for writing until after losing my husband. I met Phillip at Cedarville College, and we were married soon after graduation. We were blessed with five amazing and talented children, and so far, have five beautiful grandchildren. We lived in several different places around Ohio, and for a brief time in Connecticut and Maryland. I was primarily a stay-at-home-mom, but at times held odd jobs including, among other things, child care, substitute teaching, and school bus driving.

I love reading, spending time with my family and friends, writing my stories, and petting dogs and cats (I've had both, but currently just love on other people's pets). I enjoy the beach, sunsets, and mountains, especially when the sun is shining, and the breeze is warm. And I'm excited to see how God will lead me in the next book! Stay tuned!

Other titles in this series: **Before the Sun Sets**

Karen Kinney

Made in the USA
Middletown, DE
09 December 2025

24419859R00234